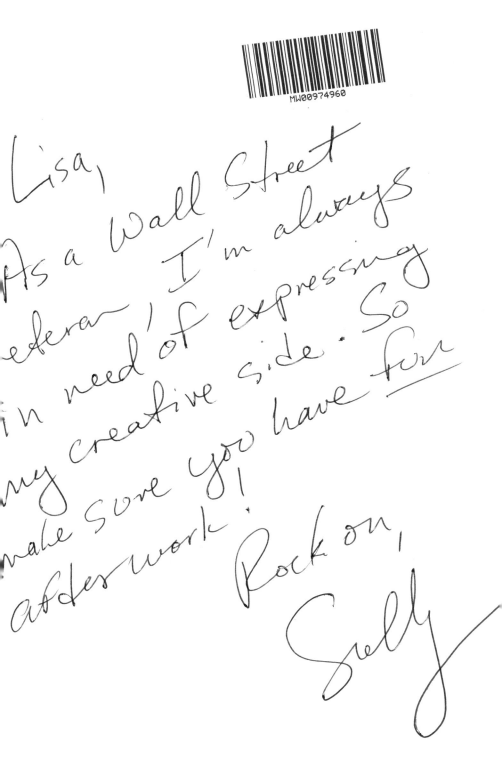

Lisa,

As a Wall Street veteran, I'm always in need of expressing my creative side. So make sure you have _fun_ after work!

Rock on,

Sally

# ROCK AND ROLL
# MURDER

# ROCK AND ROLL MURDER

John Sullivan

iUniverse, Inc.
New York  Lincoln  Shanghai

# ROCK AND ROLL MURDER

iUniverse books may be ordered through booksellers or by contacting:

iUniverse
2021 Pine Lake Road, Suite 100
Lincoln, NE 68512
www.iuniverse.com
1-800-Authors (1-800-288-4677)

ISBN-13: 978-0-595-36703-0 (pbk)
ISBN-13: 978-0-595-81271-4 (cloth)
ISBN-13: 978-0-595-81125-0 (ebk)
ISBN-10: 0-595-36703-8 (pbk)
ISBN-10: 0-595-81271-6 (cloth)
ISBN-10: 0-595-81125-6 (ebk)

Printed in the United States of America

# *Acknowledgements*

*I dedicate this book to my wife and kids,*

*to my supportive parents, and*

*to the rockers whose music has influenced me over the years:*

The Who, U2, The Jam, Nirvana, The Clash, The Beatles,

Pearl Jam, The Police, Foo Fighters, Black Sabbath,

Van Halen, The Sex Pistols, Ben Folds Five, Elvis Presley,

George Thorogood, Spinal Tap, Triumph, Jethro Tull,

Fleetwood Mac, Oasis, Stevie Ray Vaughan, Chuck Berry,

Judas Priest, Aerosmith, Billy Joel, Squeeze, Green Day,

Bob Dylan, Tom Petty and The Heartbreakers, Iron Maiden,

Jeff Beck, The Kinks, Bruce Springsteen and the E Street Band,

AC/DC, Motörhead, Cream, The Jimi Hendrix Experience,

Guns 'N Roses, The Rolling Stones, David Bowie, Queen,

Lynyrd Skynyrd, Metallica, R.E.M., Janis Joplin, The Doors,

Radiohead, Led Zeppelin, Rush, Cheap Trick, Pink Floyd,

Deep Purple, Yes, The Ramones, Elvis Costello and

the Attractions, The Pretenders, Red Hot Chili Peppers,

The Talking Heads, Genesis, Creedence Clearwater Revival,

ZZ Top, Heart, Joe Jackson, Twisted Sister, Live,

Neil Young, Rage Against The Machine, Stone Temple Pilots,

The Allman Brothers Band, Soundgarden, The Grateful Dead,

The Pogues, The Doobie Brothers, Weezer, The Eagles,

Liz Phair, Jefferson Airplane,

and the best band in the world—The John Sullivan Brigade.

# *Introduction*

There are those that love to rock, like me. And there are those that do not, like the great woman I married. This is a story for those who do.

It was 1980 when I bought my first real rock and roll instrument at Manny's Music Store in New York City on 48th Street and Broadway. If I was going to be a rocker someday, I needed to make a musical pilgrimage to the place where the famous and not so famous went rock and roll shopping.

Even though the new wave movement was the current hot sound, the classic hard rock bands were firmly entrenched in the rock world. I, of course, was raised on the guitar rocking stuff: Chuck Berry, The Who, Cream, Deep Purple, etc. But I dug any rock song as long as it had four or six strings on it. If I didn't hear anyone wailing, I wasn't listening for very long.

After some careful consideration, I was staying with the bass guitar as my rock instrument. I loved rhythm, but the drums meant I had to sit and after years of classical piano lessons, I was done sitting. I wanted to sing and jump around to the music.

When I finally arrived at Manny's one afternoon, I was very anxious. I had no idea of what I was doing or what to look for. With only $300 and little knowledge on how to buy the right instrument, I thought I would be leaving empty handed. Out of nowhere came a burly looking, longhaired salesman to assist me.

"Can I help you, kid?" he asked.

"Yeah, um, I'm looking for a bass," I said quietly.

"Uh huh. How much are you looking to spend?"

"$300."

"$300?" said the salesman. After his initial shock subsided, he walked to the back of the store, disappearing from sight. *Had I offended him?* I had no idea. Personally, I was convinced that with my small amount of cash, they were out of decent bass guitars but there was at least one crappy bass he'd try to sell me from the back of the store. But I'd take anything now as long as it came from Manny's. As I tried to figure out what I should do next, he returned with something in his hand.

"Here's a bass," the salesman said. "It's used but check it out."

What he was holding in front of me was the music industry's standard bass guitar: a mid- 1970s starburst *Fender Precision*. As I stared in shock, the salesman handed the bass to me. It was incredible. The bass had great action off the fret board, the giant machine heads were cool looking, and it was super heavy.

"Want me to plug you into an amp?" said the salesman.

"Uh, that's ok." As someone who had only been plunking away for barely a year, I was not about to embarrass myself with so many other talented musicians within earshot. I just couldn't believe I was holding a classic rock instrument in my hands. And it was all mine for a whopping $279, which included a black rectangular case that said *Fender* in silver on the outside.

"Here," I said, giving the salesman all the cash out of my pocket.

"Good luck," said the salesman.

I put the *Precision* back into the case and off I went to Penn Station to catch a train back home. The second I arrived, I ran up to my room like a kid with a brand new toy on Christmas morning. After plugging the bass into my small amplifier, the cheap amp was no match for the *Precision*. The speaker cone practically jumped out from the casing after I hit the E string. *I had arrived.* A quarter of a century later, that remarkable bass is still mine today, having used it at numerous shows in the New York City area as well as on a few CDs I have released the past several years.

But rock and roll is only part of my life. It is not my entire life. I have known others that were as entranced as I was about rock and roll back when I was a teenager, but I soon discovered that the rock world of big money issues, eccentric personalities, changing fads and the many vices was a difficult place to exist on a regular basis. The fact of the matter was I had become more set in my ways than I imagined, especially after my kids were born. But if there were a way to find a balance between those two worlds, I'd still like to know!

As a local New York area rocker who's gotten to know a few rock and roll full-timers, the pro rockers live a very different life. They are proud when their song makes kids think about the world. They feed off those concert shows where the crowd claps in unison to the beat. They often go insane in crafting a 'creative' record that will hopefully become a commercial success. They look to the past and future for opportunities to play with their idols and those they mentor in order to stay relevant. And they worry about keeping their careers going, as it can abruptly end without warning.

But they do what they do because they can. That, and the basic fact they never want to sit behind a desk or be up on a ladder like the rest of us working stiffs. They are entertainers, and want to rock and roll until the very, very end.

*John Sullivan, 2005*

# T.P. Autobio
## summary notes
## excerpts (early '80s
## section)

*After MTV started broadcasting, I was pretty much done with rock music. It wasn't that I hated playing the guitar or writing new songs but I was fed up with the constant grind of having to continue to live up to everyone's expectations. And I wasn't going to start making stupid, mindless short films of my songs for the video generation.*

*When The Winding Roads first started out back in the early Sixties, I was convinced that if we stayed together for five years and made some money, we all would have felt we were successful. Most of the bands we had followed in the Fifties had a few years of stardom and then went off to do other things, like managing bands or opening a business. No one wanted to be performing for too long. It was too much of a grind.*

*But in the mid-Sixties, when rock music exploded on both sides of the Atlantic, if you could find a champion at your record label that believed in everything you did, the least corrupt music manager you could snag, a band of ladies to keep you horny and fashionably hip, and a small legion of fanatics to keep the reporters writing about you, basically you were golden. Of course, you had to keep pumping out the tunes. We knew bands weaker than us who were great marketers and were making money faster than we were!*

*By the late Seventies, however, the writing was on the wall. Punk music woke up all of the big rock music companies and after MTV started broadcasting, we were officially 'old farts.' Profitable farts, mind you, but just not relevant farts. Worse, as our generation of fans got older, they wanted us to stay young by continuing to churn out only the 'greatest hits' songs. Once during the '81 <u>Moonshine</u> tour, I announced that we were doing a new song from the latest record and this one guy in the front started yelling 'BOOOOO! Play the old stuff, Tommy! Play the old stuff!' I shouted down to him, 'Why don't you come up here and play the old stuff?' Others in his guy's section started to boo along with him. I threw my guitar into the crowd, gave them the finger and walked off the stage.*

*From day one, I have viewed myself as an artist who's always wanted to try something different. I think part of our early success as a band was that we always tried to challenge ourselves, even if the label was complaining that they weren't hearing any "hits" off the demos. Trying something new is what sets the great bands apart from the good bands. Because at some point in a long career, you will dread playing certain songs that you've literally played a thousand times. But for the person in the audience that never saw you before, you feel you have an obligation to perform those songs like it's the first time you've ever done them. Playing that new material was critical in keeping my sanity.*

*When I decided that I could no longer commit myself to the band on a full-time basis, everybody was upset with me. I finally understood how Paul McCartney felt when he was the first to announce he was leaving The Beatles. Quickly I was hearing things from fans like 'how could you do this to us?' Even my band mates were puzzled. They were enjoying the money flow and weren't that interested in changing direction at all.*

*But I didn't want to be the guitarist in The Winding Roads for the rest of my life. That's the thing about being successful in the entertainment industry. Once they've got you pegged as something, that's it. They don't want you going off and discovering new things. As part of the public domain, they feel that they own you forever. And that's it.*

*Except that's NOT it. I still remember what it was like to be an unknown in the music industry. In the early days when I was trying to make it in rock and roll, I was also dabbling with folk and jazz and blues with friends and acquaintances I bumped into on the streets of New York City. It was a great time in my life. I felt as if I could do anything I wanted to and for as long as I wanted to. No one had me labeled as anything in music yet so I ventured into anything that tickled my fancy.*

*Once you become famous, it's so difficult to leave the past, otherwise known to most fans as "the glory days." Don't get me wrong; I'm grateful for the career I have had in the music biz and the wealth that it brought me. But there have been times when I wished I could start over again in a totally different direction—just writing and playing a new kind of music to people who were unaware of who I was.*

# CHAPTER 1

▼

"Hey! Hey Tommy! Over here! Can you sign this for me?" a man yelled.

Tommy Peterson stopped walking for a brief second. He was relieved that the induction ceremony for the 2004 Rock and Roll Hall of Fame was done and the onstage live jam that was happening was winding down. The museum's board members had asked the New York rock legend since last year to attend this year's function. It was the 35th anniversary of his band's landmark record, The Winding Roads' *Everything Is Nothing*, and they wanted to pay tribute to the recording. Peterson accepted the plaque but was hoping to sneak out undetected during the jam. Unfortunately, he had to answer his loudmouth fan.

"Not today," replied the aging rocker as he continued to move towards the hotel's revolving doors. The graying, black-haired man groaned as he headed away from the desperate autograph seeker. But the portly man was still closing in at full speed from inside The Waldorf-Astoria's lobby, making a direct beeline to the veteran rock star.

A couple of decades ago, Peterson's cutting-edge rock band was at the top of the rock and roll world. Back then, the band's entourage would have never let a renegade fan get so close. But in 2004, the rock world was now playing second fiddle to the hip-hop generation—not unlike what the jazz world was like when it surrendered to rock back in the Seventies. And there didn't seem to be a need for a bodyguard for an old rocker now eligible for Social Security. Only this lone oddball in the main lobby remembered the millions of records Peterson's band had sold during their career.

"Come on, man, I'm a huge fan of yours," barked the gentleman. The rambling fan, who looked to be somewhere near his late forties, had an all-access pass dangling from his sweaty neck. He was also lumbering around with an oversized canvas bag jammed with rock and roll paraphernalia that had been handed out prior to tonight's event. "I've got all The Roads' albums and even some of your solo CDs. Can't you just sign this bag? Look! I got Jackson Browne's and Bruce Springsteen's autograph tonight. Can you just sign…"

At 58, the New York City guitarist had grown weary of unfamiliar faces. In the early days, Peterson had been working on some demos in his bedroom when a deranged fan broke into his apartment, locked Peterson and his family in a bathroom, and stole his demo tapes along with a couple of rare guitars and some cash. After 40 years of performing, that home invasion episode was all Peterson needed to remind him about keeping his distance.

"No!" replied Peterson, refusing to even look back at the annoying fan and his signature-covered bag. Peterson never understood what the value was in having his sloppy signature on anything; most of his 'chicken scratch' was practically illegible on the various surfaces they would ask him to write on. And what was the point in getting a signature? Was there a covert group of forgers disguised as music fans that were writing phony checks around the world?

"Oh, you know, no wonder everybody thinks you're such a jerk off, man," said the disgruntled fan, dropping his bag in disgust. "Why don't you put out another crappy solo CD and see who buys it this time other than me?"

The gentleman's elevated voice had now intensified, getting the attention of the busy security guards that were sprinkled throughout the ornate lobby. They were now moving towards the obnoxious fan as Peterson turned to address him directly.

"Well, how about if I write JERKOFF in block letters on your precious bag? Will that work for you?"

The fan was startled by Peterson's response. Then, the man chuckled. "Would you write that, Tommy? That…would be UNBELIEVABLE!"

A small grin appeared on Peterson's face. His first reaction had been to walk through the doors and not give the fan the satisfaction. Instead, Peterson turned back towards the persistent fellow. He decided to take the "high road" for the millionth time and give the fan what he requested. By now, the security group had surrounded both men, comfortable in knowing the rock star was safe and the fan was an excited music industry executive. Still, no one moved until the autograph signing was finished.

"Sorry about what I said, Tommy. Your music means a lot to me," said the gentleman, who handed a security guard his camera so he could have a photo of Peterson signing the bag for the fan.

"Yup," said Peterson, scribbling JERKOFF and then his signature underneath it. "Now you've got a story to go with your goodie bag."

"Oh man oh man oh man," proclaimed the fan as he began to admire the newly-written block letters. "This is soooo cool. Thank you so much!"

Peterson turned away without shaking his hand as the over-zealous attendee was being reprimanded by one of the security officers for his behavior. As Peterson headed through the revolving doors, the old rocker could hear the man yelling back at the security officer, telling him who he was and that he better "back off" unless HE wanted to lose his job at the hotel.

Although Peterson didn't bother having a security detail assigned to him, the rocker was wealthy enough to have a limo driver pick him up near Park Avenue's most famous hotel. His long-time driver Papa was waiting for him as always, just two blocks south of the event in order to avoid the constant traffic gridlock outside the hotel.

"You ok, Tommy? You seem a bit upset?" said Papa, as he opened the door for the weary Peterson.

"Nah, I'm fine. Just some loser pestering me to sign some stupid tote bag of his," said Peterson as he collapsed into the cold leather seats. "You know I almost made it out of there without having to bother with somebody but it never fails. There's always one pain in the ass at every single thing I go to."

"Sorry to hear that. You rarely ever get a break on that side, do ya?" said Papa.

Peterson smiled back at his driver. The leather-dressed Papa (his first name was Joe but he never bothered to use it) was in his early fifties and had acted as one of The Winding Roads' tour managers back in the Seventies and a small-sized body-guard on occasion. A diehard fan, Papa stayed on as Peterson's driver and assistant on the occasional Tommy Peterson solo tour after the band became inactive. Papa was well aware of Peterson's impatience towards his fans' endless requests, so he did a lot of listening.

"You would think after not recording a band record in 15 years and a solo record in seven, they just wouldn't care any-more. But there's always one in the crowd somewhere with a million questions," said Peterson. "Simply incredible."

"So are we headed over to Bowie's party now?" said Papa.

"Just drop me off at home. I'll call David tomorrow and we'll maybe do lunch somewhere soon. I'm just not in the mood," said Peterson.

Peterson enjoyed Bowie's get-togethers and others thrown by resident veteran New York rockers such as Lou Reed and Billy Joel but only when he was up for it. Although admired by many current rockers, his status as a Sixties rock icon fit in much better at the 'over 40' parties. A couple of years ago, Peterson had been invited to a Puff Daddy function at his East Hampton mansion at the end of Long Island. During the party, Peterson was cornered on a couple of occasions by security if the old man actually had an invitation to be there at the hip-hop party.

That minor inconvenience didn't bother Peterson half as much as when he waited forever to get a beer at a mini-bar with several gorgeous young women standing around him—without one of them saying a word to him. Back in his prime, the rock star legend would literally have had to fight the girls off. At this kind of party, however, Peterson was virtually invisible. It certainly wasn't the end of the world but just a different one he had been accustomed to.

The black limousine slowly pulled up in front of the tony West Village three-story brownstone, located just a block off of Hudson Street. The late 19<sup>th</sup> century residence he had purchased and restored back in the mid-Seventies, back when the general public had ignored the neighborhood, was a perfect fit for the long-time New York resident. The surroundings reminded him of his idyllic days in suburbia where everyone knew everyone: the long-time residents, the familiar merchants, and the same cops walking their beat. And the quality of life was surprisingly good for a major city. The uptown lifestyle was never Tommy's cup of tea.

Rising real estate prices, however, were now driving away many young, working families and bringing in pretentious Hollywood types and annoying Wall Street know-it-alls. It was becoming way too chic and upscale for his earthy tastes. The days of having nearby friends passing by on the street and inviting them up to hear his latest tunes into the wee hours of the night were long gone. Peterson wasn't lonely, but without steady gigs or a planned tour, his ex-wife and children relocated out to California and his girlfriend frequently at some fundraising event, it wasn't a busy time for the veteran rock star.

Peterson sauntered through the door, picked up his mail and then pressed the UP button to the two-person elevator he had installed several years ago. The wear and tear from the endless tours, the jumping around onstage, and just being 58 meant the knees and ankles would not work well on the multiple sets of staircases. The extra pounds he had put on in recent years weren't helping. Peterson's only exercise came from the stationary bike inside his third floor studio sanctuary—the only place he could record and listen to his 'music in progress' without interruption.

Because of the late evening's gala, Peterson had told his part-time engineer Kevin 'KK' Kelly to take the night off. There was no need to pay KK for no reason. Besides, Peterson knew how to work most of the basic playback operations: stop, rewind, and play. All he wanted to hear tonight was the rough song mixes slated for his upcoming solo CD. Peterson wanted to get his ears back in shape for the remixing and remastering of The Winding Roads' sixth CD, *Black Wine And Red Nights*. But Peterson wasn't in the mood for the oldies just yet. That project would be addressed after his solo CD was completed. For him, the new music was always as important as the old.

As the elevator door opened up quietly to the third floor, Peterson stepped out and towards the large wooden studio door. Out from the shadows, the veteran rocker felt a hand landing unexpectedly on his shoulder. Peterson gasped, throwing himself up against the nearby wall. The initial shock of someone hiding in his hallway temporarily paralyzed him and was unable to speak. Recognizing the unkempt man standing in front of him, Peterson remained frozen in a total state of confusion.

"How…how the hell did you get up here?" asked Peterson.

The unexpected guest replied, "Your past has finally caught up with mine, Tommy."

# Chapter 2

---▼---

Tony Russo was not a good morning person but today was worse than usual.

With his ears ringing constantly from last night's jam, the well-known veteran rock writer and critic had been out partying late that night with several groups of people, such as musicians, industry folks, writers, movie stars and politicians, after the Hall of Fame gala was concluded. It was part of the job.

After writing about rock music for over 30 years, Russo was amazed by how he was able to hold a conversation with such diverse entertainment personalities. However, Russo was unable to hold his liquor like he could in the early days and his chronic hearing problems was not helping. So as the sunshine crept through the blinds and onto his face, Russo was one miserable guest.

"What is with these stupid things?" yelled Russo as he hurled a pillow towards the window blinds. Upon impact, the blinds unfurled completely, allowing multiple streams of sunlight to pour in from every angle. Russo pulled the covers over his head. He had already turned off his cell phone, took the room phone off the hook, hung a DO NOT DISTURB sign outside the door and was rooming alone. Why couldn't he just get a little cooperation today?

Russo peeked at his watch. It was 9:15 am and checkout time was listed at 11. It was just enough time for a quick shower, a walk outside, and some breakfast before heading back home to his house in Rockville Centre on Long Island. It was nice that the rock music magazine he was working for was gracious enough to let him stay overnight in Manhattan, even though his house was barely an hour away. Russo worked from home a great deal of the time, so he knew his wife and kids would understand if Daddy chose to stay in the Big Apple for one night.

After brushing his teeth, Russo stared at his face in the semi-fogged bathroom mirror. At 51, the wavy hair was still coming through his tender scalp but the hair colors were definitely changing. His Irish and Russian face was neither as smooth nor as thin as it was a few years ago. The blue green eyes looked puffy as well but it was not from being out late with the teen rockers or the veteran rollers. For Tony Russo, it was merely time catching up to the three decades' worth of rock and roll music living.

As one might expect, Russo's queen-sized hotel bed resembled a typical journalist's untidiness, completely covered by music magazines, candy wrappers, CDs and every New York City newspaper available. Underneath the clutter was his brand new Mini iPod, which had a whopping seven songs (out of a possible 1,000) downloaded so far.

Russo was still clinging on to his CD player and his travel pack of classic CDs that were all labeled "Stranded On An Island Music." It was a collection of rock music that he needed to survive:

*The Who: Quadrophenia*
*Nirvana: Nevermind*
*The Clash: London Calling*
*Jimi Hendrix Experience: Are You Experienced?*
*The Kinks: One For The Road*
*The Beatles: Abbey Road*
*Bruce Springsteen: Born To Run*
*Foo Fighters: The Colour and The Shape*
*Led Zeppelin: I*
*The Jam: All Mod Cons*
*The Rolling Stones: Sticky Fingers*
*Ben Folds Five: Whatever and Ever Amen*
*Black Sabbath: Paranoid*

Although tempted to slip in a CD he bought yesterday by The Carpenters, his 'secret' non-rock favorite artist, Russo placed the *Quadrophenia* CD into his player. He often thought back to his "trial by fire" entrance into rock music reporting when he had to tag along one night with The Who's legendary drummer Keith Moon during their *Who's Next* tour. His editor at the time gave the teenager an open-ended assignment to not only review the concert but to follow the late drummer afterwards. At five-foot-ten and 160 pounds, Russo had to battle through hordes of aggressive groupies, uncooperative roadies and other unsavory characters just to keep up with Moon.

But the drummer befriended Russo and gave him plenty of copy for his article, entitled "A Night Out With Keith Moon— Run For Your Lives!" The Who's management was not thrilled at his article, which contained lurid details about the evening. However, a couple of weeks later Russo received a signed note from The Who's bassist John Entwistle asking why Russo left out the evening's best parts.

The assignments never got easier after that story appeared, as Russo's ability to tackle a wide variety of rock and roll personalities and deliver great copy only got his editors more excited about giving him the next story. Russo loved writing but he first tried to make it as a singer and guitarist in a band during the late Sixties. But his efforts never amounted to nothing more than a few shows and a vinyl 45 single indie pressing that went unnoticed. Still, the rock and roll world intrigued Russo, as he soon discovered he had a flair for writing about the music he loved. The performing career ended but a rock and roll writing career began. And the rest was history.

Russo, however, knew that he was at a turning point in his 30-year music writing career. He still had bills to pay but it was time to slow things down and find a better way to make a living. Russo was pretty much finished with rock right after Kurt Cobain of Nirvana fame exited this world via his shotgun back in 1994. As a rock guitar aficionado, he did not identify with hip-hop, electronica or boy bands. It wasn't that he hated

Tupac Shakur, Moby or The Backstreet Boys but Russo didn't understand where they were coming from—and he didn't care. Giving press coverage to his rock friends' solo efforts, such as Alan Parsons, Mark Farner and Ricky Byrd, was more enjoyable than listening to the other alternatives that were out there.

Rock events like last night's gala were a bit confusing for Russo. There were soul, pop, country, jazz, and hip hop people in attendance and the veteran rock critic wasn't quite sure why. To him, rock and roll was only about loud guitars, big drums and screaming singers. But every year, with more and more crossover artists coming in and out of the 'rock' format, Russo thought the museum might soon have to change its name to something more appropriate, like The Rock and Roll (And Various Other Genres) Hall of Fame and Museum.

Examining his hastily scribbled notes from the previous night, Russo wondered how far he would have to go to create an article that would excite both his publisher and the magazine's audience. Russo remembered when Black Sabbath's singer Ozzy Osbourne said he never grasped why any hardened rock and roller would care about getting inducted into something like a hall of fame.

But many of the classic rockers Russo grew up with had passed away and those who remained were getting very long in the tooth. And the difficult, uncompromising rock survivors, Russo believed, were quite pleased that their rock and roll contributions from years past would be displayed for future generations to come. Yes, the same ornery rockers that had remained in a state of arrested development wanted to bring their extended family to a place that showcased their musical contribution to society.

*Who would have thought rock and roll would have come to this?* Russo thought to himself. *Certainly not rock DJ legend Alan Freed back in '52.* And definitely not long time rock snob Tony Russo in 2004.

After forcing some of his already wrinkled clothes into his overnight travel bag, Russo passed on ordering up room service and headed on out the door. He thought about calling into the offices of *Rock Forever* magazine, the relatively new NYC monthly startup with a terrible name that was paying Russo, to find out if there was anything else he needed to do for this article.

But he didn't care much for the magazine, knowing they were always trying to take advantage of a recently unemployed journalist. Russo's first article for them had been a feature on a rock and roll fantasy camp, an outing geared for adults with varied music skills that wanted to play "rock star" for a few days. Russo trailed two of the 80 campers, who shelled out several thousand dollars, who then got placed in a band, received music instructions from veteran rockers, took in performances from the same resident pros, and were given the unique opportunity to perform live at a major club.

At first, Russo thought the assignment was a bit odd after learning the rock pros were actually required to whip these music novices into shape. In the end, however, the rock writer snob discovered the seasoned rockers enjoyed bridging the gap with their long-time fans. And the smiles Russo witnessed on the campers' faces on the final night were ones that were probably non-existent at their respective workplaces.

That, in essence, was the primary goal of the magazine Russo was currently writing for—to maintain the classic rock bond between veteran artist and rock fan. And his boss Johnny Merseburg IV believed in that concept every single day. The wealthy Connecticut publisher of *Rock Forever* had more money to burn on almost anything he wanted. As a diehard Bob Dylan, The Band, and Grateful Dead music fanatic, he had always dreamed of launching his own newsstand magazine that focused only on music acts prior to August 1, 1981—the first day that MTV began broadcasting. With the one-time playboy a regular visitor to The Rock and Roll Museum, covering an event that included dozens of classic rockers from beginning to end was Merseburg's kind of feature article. That's why Tony Russo was here.

But the disorganized reporter decided it was not yet time to call into the office, opting instead to pick up his free newspaper in front of his door as he exited the room. Russo had not turned on his cell phone; worse, he never bothered to look over at his hotel phone. The yellow message light was blinking feverishly. A call had apparently come in during his shower but he never retrieved the message that awaited him.

Standing by the seventh floor elevator, Russo pulled out his new cell phone from his pants pocket. He was proud he had learned how to use the text messaging service on the phone but could not seem to get a connection inside the hotel at the moment. There were a couple of email messages left for him, but Russo decided to wait until he got downstairs to listen to them. As the elevator doors opened up, a middle-aged couple carrying tote bags from last night's event were already chatting away. Russo could tell from the expensive clothes they were wearing that they had more money than God. Anyone other than Russo who stayed at this posh five-star hotel had to be in the "stinking rich" category.

"I can't believe it. It's quite shocking, you know. He was so young," said the woman as she continued to put her makeup on inside the elevator.

"Yeah," replied her husband. "But even though crime is down in New York City, there's still crazy people floating around."

"Honey, make sure I get a newspaper before we get in the cab. It should have his picture on the cover."

"Ok. If not, probably those throwaway daily newspapers I saw yesterday will have it. They usually get those stories right away."

Russo had no idea of whom they were talking about but he didn't want to be nosy. It was his own fault for not turning on the television or checking the Internet on his laptop. His guess was that it was another young movie star that got in over their head. But he didn't care much for those tabloid stories. Russo had plenty of work to do other than reading about the latest Hollywood fatality.

The elevator doors opened to the main lobby and a ton of TV cameras aimed in every direction, with their bright lights blasting throughout the open space. Russo could see a number of reporters covering some event live from the hotel's lobby and were making quite a commotion. Russo was completely in the dark as to what was all the commotion in the packed lobby.

"Wow!" said the woman as the three of them stepped out of the elevator. "This is incredible. I had no idea Tommy Peterson's murder would get this kind of media coverage."

# CHAPTER 3

▼

"What did you just say?" said an exasperated Russo.

The blond-haired woman turned to Russo. "Tommy Peterson's dead. You know, the guitarist from The Winding Roads. He was murdered in his studio last night after being here at the Hall of Fame show. They just found him. And guess what? I actually saw him last night here at the hotel. Right here!"

Russo was speechless. *Tommy Peterson was dead.* His heart started to race as the unexpected news of the tragedy sunk in. The writer had known Tommy Peterson for years and had become good friends ever since he did a long, in-depth interview in 1974 following the death of one of Peterson's ex-band mates. When bassist Steve Mars was unable to perform due to his heavy drug use, both parties thought it was best that Mars should leave the band. A month after Mars left, police found his frozen body underneath a tree, wearing only a pair of shorts. Mars' death was ruled "accidental" by the coroner, but Peterson was quietly singled out as the one who pushed Mars to his ultimate demise.

But Peterson used the interview as an opportunity to explain what happened, while Russo weaved interesting other rock historical references into the article, like how Mick Jagger and Keith Richards of The Rolling Stones had fingers pointed at them after Brian Jones' suspicious 1969 death shortly after exiting their band.

After Russo's acclaimed article was published, most people believed that Mars not only left on his own but also was responsible for his own destructive path. Russo, indirectly, had bailed out Peterson from further criticism. Extremely grateful for the supportive article, Peterson became close friends with Russo as a result, sharing thoughts and staying in close contact over the next three decades. With Tommy's unexpected death, however, there was nothing left for them to share.

"When did...oh boy. I gotta call somebody," said Russo.

"Are you okay, honey? You don't look well," said the woman.

"I just have to sit down somewhere. I feel lousy."

Scanning the area, Russo spotted an oversized leather chair that he could hide in and left the woman. His mind continued to race in a million different directions. Russo knew Peterson wasn't revered in the same way as the great Bob Dylan but Tommy was a bonafide rock legend, and it was a big deal that he was gone. Many in the industry agreed Peterson was an insightful songwriter and a talented guitarist, a US version of

The Kinks' Ray Davies. Russo recalled Peterson once telling him he was most proud of the fact that his US-based rock band stayed on the Billboard music charts throughout the various British rock band waves. Getting that American sound around the world was important to Peterson.

Russo reached back into his pocket for his cell phone. "I gotta call my wife," he mumbled to himself. The rock critic dialed his wife Jeanne nervously, even though he had not yet checked any of the messages that had been left on his cell phone.

"Tony!" answered his wife of twenty-four years. "Where are you? Didn't you get my message this morning about Tommy? Why was your cell phone off?"

"Oh, for crying out loud, Jeanne, don't start giving me a lecture! I just found out a minute ago. I didn't want to be bothered and then I forgot to check. Man, I cannot believe this."

"Did you see Tommy at all last night?" said Jeanne.

"Yeah, briefly. You know Tommy hated these events. As soon as he got his plaque, I talked with him and then he headed towards the lobby and out the door. He told me he was going to Bowie's party afterwards but I never saw him there. I guess he decided not to go. God! I should have called him!"

"I don't think that would have mattered," said Jeanne. "You know for a fact that Tommy did whatever he wanted. How many times did you have to call him back to get in touch with him?"

Russo agreed. "But I guess I gotta call my boss. He's going to want some copy on this real soon, especially knowing that they are going to print any day."

"Just take a deep breath and get yourself together," said Jeanne. "Come on home as soon as you can."

"I'll call you back later. I'm going to see if I can find out more about this. This is unbelievable," replied Russo.

Russo slipped the cell phone back into his jacket and began to walk around the lobby, trying to listen in on what some of the local TV broadcasters were saying. Russo speculated that the vast majority of the reporters in the crowded space were born around the time The Winding Roads were wrapping up their career, so they wouldn't have much to say off the top of their heads about Tommy Peterson. As Russo heard the words "tied up" and "stabbed" being used, he spotted a crumpled copy of a daily free newspaper on a table. Russo quickly claimed it and focused directly on today's headline:

## ROCK AND ROLL MURDER
### *NYC Rock Icon*
### *Tommy Peterson Murdered*

The bold newspaper headline made Russo's stomach queasy, although the famous photo of Peterson in mid-flight off the drum riser with his *Fender Stratocaster* way above his head made him smile a little. He turned to page 3 to find out the details of the murder. Although Russo's own story would be more about the past than the present, he needed to find out what had happened to his talented rock and roll friend:

"New York rock and roll music icon Tommy Peterson was found murdered inside his Manhattan apartment studio early this morning. The well known New York guitarist and songwriter of The Winding Roads was just 58 years old. Born in Queens on April 7, 1948, Tommy loved music from the beginning, starting with piano lessons at the age…"

Russo stopped reading for a moment. Editing some of Peterson's nearly completed autobiography, with the working title of *Looking Back Down Those Roads,* gave him access to more information about the rocker than anyone cared to know. *Of all the stories for him to write,* thought Russo, *the biggest story about Tommy was the only story he would never be able to share.* He skipped farther down to locate the gruesome details. As always, there was plenty of descriptive copy about the crime scene in the city's papers:

"Insiders close to the scene indicated that Peterson was apparently tied down, stabbed repeatedly in the chest, then impaled by the blunt end of an electric guitar. In addition, a bank of speakers was placed in a circle around Peterson, indicating to some that the beloved rocker might have fallen prey to some sort of local ritualistic cult."

The cult reference baffled the seasoned rock reporter. *What was up with the guitar and the circle of amps?* He was a non-practicing Roman Catholic and that was the extent of it. There were no direct tie-ins to religion in any of his music that would draw in some freaky local cult. But Russo was aware the story had just come out and considering that there were no suspects at the time, there was probably little information but tons of speculation. The police, as always, were not saying much at all.

Russo yanked the page out about the late Tommy Peterson from the cheaply made newspaper and chucked the rest of it under a small table. He kicked the side of the hotel wall and then placed his forehead against the cold wall. It didn't make any sense at all to Russo. How could the biggest rock performer he personally knew in the music business end up like this? Tommy Peterson was a rock legend for almost 40 years and some heartless killer snuffed out his entire life overnight.

The rock critic was overcome with sadness, as Tony Russo's grief for his late friend was clearly evident to anyone standing in the hotel lobby.

And someone was.

# CHAPTER 4

▼

Detective Caitlin O'Connell had just finished up with a gang-related murder case in Staten Island when she received an early morning call about Tommy Peterson's murder. In a nanosecond, the slender-looking brunette left for the West Village.

Although O'Connell had only been a New York City homicide detective for three years, the feisty Irishwoman born and raised in Ridgewood in the NYC borough of Queens had been on the force for almost two decades. She dutifully followed her father, uncle and brother's footsteps by becoming a New York City police officer after graduating from nearby St. John's University in the heart of Jamaica, Queens. O'Connell realized most of her friends heading into teaching, law school or Wall Street. But the hyperactive teenager had promised her strict mother that she would first get a college education before becoming a cop. Gloria believed it was something for her only daughter to fall back on just in case.

But at 39, O'Connell was starting to feel her age after learning her favorite rocker was dead. During her high school and college days, O'Connell had fronted her own rock band, using tough-sounding, women-fronted rock bands like Heart and The Pretenders as blueprints for what she wanted to be like. However, The Winding Roads was her all-time favorite band and Peterson was the one rocker she identified with more than anyone else. The crass local rocker had the hard looks, songwriting ability, high energy and New York attitude all wrapped up in one rock and roll package. O'Connell met Tommy Peterson briefly in 1982 at an in-store record signing down at J&R Music across the street from City Hall. Signing a solo record Peterson was promoting at the time, 'Nice to meet you' was all that Peterson said to O'Connell. But that was all that Tommy's PR handlers would allow. Today, however, O'Connell had unlimited access to him. But it was not exactly what she had in mind.

The detective walked through the sad-looking crowds outside Peterson's West Village residence, as people were spilling out down the block and onto Hudson Street. Various groups were leaving bouquets of flowers and small, white candles outside his place. It was obvious that many folks were visibly upset by the tragic news. Along the length of Peterson's block, fans and mourners alike began singing songs with the various acoustic guitarists that were popping up every ten feet. O'Connell recognized a song they were singing from one of her favorite Winding Roads albums:

> *No matter where we are, friend, you are here*
> *No matter where we are now, you are near*

Although the distressed crowds weren't like the hysterical drama that the 1980 murder of The Beatles' John Lennon brought in front of The Dakota and nearby Central Park, Peterson's horrific murder was still another great Sixties rocker lost forever under tragic circumstances. As O'Connell flashed her detective badge and entered the former rocker's apartment, she was probably the only officer there who could identify almost every rock and roll item displayed inside Peterson's home.

As O'Connell stepped inside, Peterson's main floor resembled a small rock and roll museum—except that it was also someone's entire life on display. Everyone knew Tommy Peterson was not a 'remember the old times' guy but he apparently had some attachments to a few items from his rock and roll past. In a framed box on the wall, there was the orange oversized Gretsch guitar that Peterson had partially set on fire at the Altamont Speedway concert debacle back in '69. Hanging on two nails driven into the wall was the red, white and blue-fringed jacket covered with small white skulls that Peterson wore in their controversial 1976 tour documentary film, *Our Country*.

But O'Connell's favorite item in Peterson's apartment was different than anything else she had seen in a NYC residence. Peterson had a rare 1960s Vox AC-30 Top Boost guitar amplifier—which The Beatles had made 'famous' during their first tour—dangling from the ceiling on a thick, swinging rope. From the damaged look of the vintage amp, it was quite evident the guitarist would attack it occasionally with a nearby baseball bat as if the amp was some sort of everlasting piñata. *That*, O'Connell thought, *was just weird.*

Cutting short her personal rock and roll museum tour, O'Connell rode the private elevator up to the third floor studio.

As she rode the elevator alone, the detective braced herself for what she was about to see. Her one weakness from working on the force was murder scenes that involved multiple stabbings. Gunshots were often just one or two isolated holes while strangulations or suffocations were invisible. But any crime scene that had a victim who had been stabbed repeatedly made O'Connell ill. Because the knife was a silent weapon, the detective learned early on that it allowed an attacker to assault someone numerous times. The end result was something she never got comfortable with.

The elevator door slid open and standing in front of her was her close friend and fellow detective Steve Glover. An older but more experienced detective than O'Connell, Glover was also a long time friend of O'Connell's family.

"Caitlin, straight through here," said Glover.

O'Connell stepped under the yellow DO NOT ENTER tape and entered Tommy Peterson's home recording studio. Upon first glance, O'Connell noticed Peterson had affixed all of his gold and platinum records onto the multi-colored walls. In between the framed gold and platinum records were fantastic, large-sized photographs of Peterson and some of the biggest people in rock and roll he had met throughout his storied career. But O'Connell's eyes shifted to her favorite rock star in the center of the room.

"Wow," mumbled O'Connell. "I cannot believe this."

There was Tommy Peterson, crumpled deep inside a giant black chair, partially bound and gagged with multiple stab wounds and a rare Gibson Flying V guitar neck sticking half way out from the center of his chest. Surrounding the chair in a circle was a dozen vintage amplifiers of various sizes, along with pictures of the ancient Stonehenge ruins in England tossed about the floor. As O'Connell looked over the crime scene, she could overhear a bizarre conversation that made her blood boil.

"Hey, you know how much that Flying V guitar was worth?" said one member of the forensic team to a cop standing guard over the room. Apparently O'Connell wasn't the only one who had been in a rock and roll band.

"Look at that craftsmanship and that fret board. Man, that was one incredible…"

"Hey!" shouted O'Connell, "I know how much it's worth. It WAS a rare guitar. Who cares? It's sticking out of someone's chest! So shut your mouth, do your work and have some respect."

"Sorry," said the assistant medical examiner. "I just never saw one of those guitars up close."

"Yeah, well get a look at it because it's going to the evidence room," shot back O'Connell. Peterson's studio was covered in classic rock memorabilia but this wasn't a pawnshop or an auction at Sotheby's. It was the place where her idol lived, made music, and died a horrible death. It was a murder scene and the detective owed it to the victim to maintain some sort of decorum.

Glover signaled for O'Connell to head over to the front of the monitor board. She stared at a picture on the wall showing legendary studio man Jimmy Lorenzo, who had worked at The Hit Factory for years, building the home studio they were now standing in. Peterson's home studio had a nice blend of both the old analog and new digital world of professional recording: a smart-looking Neve 8068 Mark II console with "flying faders", a pristine Studer A80 24-track tape recorder, the most recent Apple Power Mac G5 computer complete with ProTools, and a ton of other equipment that was way beyond O'Connell's music knowledge.

"Caitlin, we left the body as is until you got here. We found bloodstains on the control panel. We're also taking boot prints. Definitely a man by the size and type of boot," said Glover.

"Ok. And judging from all the lights that are on, it looks like music was running in here. Let's see what they were listening to," said O'Connell. There were two CD cases open. One of them was marked FINAL MIX and the other was marked TKAA. But only one CD was in the carousel. The power was on with a CD already in the machine but set on Pause. O'Connell pressed down on the Play button.

In a second, the entire studio sounded like four jet engines from a commercial plane that had been turned on at full blast. One cop, sleepily leaning against the door, had fallen backwards into the hallway from the deafening music. The song was the live version of The Who's 'Won't Get Fooled Again' from *The Kids Are Alright* soundtrack. Knowing that the famous Mod band from the UK once held the record for the loudest rock concert in the world, there had to be a reason why this music was set at such a high volume. O'Connell quickly hit the Pause button again.

"Jeez Louise! Why in God's name was that up so loud?" said Glover as he shook his head.

"The sound of a knife cutting into a body doesn't make much noise at all," replied O'Connell. "Maybe our psychopath hung around a bit here and decided to crank some tunes while he was committing the crime?"

"Could be, Caitlin. Or blocking out the screams before he got taped up. The entire floor's covered with pictures of Stonehenge. That means nothing to me. Maybe that note we found on Peterson has some sort of connection to the photos?" said Glover.

"What note?" said O'Connell.

Glover read the piece of paper found on Peterson out loud:

**Aggression unchallenged is aggression unleashed.**

"Does that ring a bell?" said Glover. "I'm lost."

O'Connell agreed. She had no theory either on why the murderer wrote that line for them to read, the circle of amps around the victim's chair or what all the postcards meant. One thing was certain. The detective was leaning towards a strong man who could handle the volatile Peterson. This was also not looking like a robbery. Peterson's wallet was full of cash with all his credit cards intact.

"I'm not sure what to think yet. Feels like only one person, Steve. But make sure no one turns off anything here, including the computer," said O'Connell. "We need to double check everything here to see if there's anything that might make things a bit more clear."

As O'Connell pulled out her ringing cell phone, she took one last look at her rock idol as Tommy Peterson was placed carefully inside a long, rectangular body bag for the trip down to the coroner's office. The call was from someone on The Waldorf-Astoria security team asking her to come over as soon as possible. They were keeping a close eye on one individual sitting in the lobby who might have been with Peterson at last night's show.

There was no time for O'Connell to wait for the slow-moving private elevator, as the detective ran down the three flights of stairs and into her unmarked police car.

# CHAPTER 5

▼

The emotionless, unshaven murderer sat in front of his small television in the dark, listening to the local news coverage of the Tommy Peterson murder. His fantasy had become reality and it was all playing out on the small screen.

"...At 58, Peterson was enjoying both his successful past and recent triumphs," said the TV broadcaster. "But that has now all come to an end with the discovery of his body early this morning."

*What recent triumphs?* thought the murderer. *Surely the reporter must be kidding. No one was buying those lousy solo efforts that dear old Tommy was endlessly laboring over year after year.* The killer knew *Open Window* went platinum two decades ago but the rest of Peterson's solo efforts barely sold more that 25,000 units after that. However, 25,000 CDs times $12 was a decent living and more than the murderer could even imagine making in the music industry.

As the wanted man continued to watch the old black and white footage of Tommy Peterson, he played along with his electric guitar to whatever song that came through the speakers. It didn't matter whether it was a chord or a solo. He knew the songs well enough that he could improvise right on the spot. Visible on the dirty TV screen were thin streaks of spit that had been hurled from the murderer during the first news broadcast about the dead rocker. Even though he had finished taking care of Tommy Peterson, the killer's anger was far from gone.

"...And as other artists such as The Beatles with *Sgt. Pepper's* and The Who with *Tommy* were expanding their musical boundaries, so did The Winding Roads with the release of their concept album *Everything Is Nothing* and...."

*NOT THAT PIECE OF CRAP ALBUM AGAIN,* bellowed the murderer. *How many times do I have to hear about that poorly recorded, over hyped record? The Beach Boys' Brian Wilson's reworked masterpiece 'Smile' made its rightful return this year after three decades. But that lousy Winding Roads record? ENOUGH ALREADY!* The killer was steadfast in his belief that The Roads were simply at the right place at the right time and were living off their giant publicity machine that their management group ran like a well-oiled car engine.

The angry murderer cocked his arm back and hurled his guitar forward, sending a beautiful vintage Gibson Les Paul Black Beauty straight into the wall. Ignoring the damage he made to the guitar and the wall, he reached over for a bottle of whiskey as he admired a small, framed picture he had put on a coffee table. It was the fugitive himself standing next to members of the legendary UK band The Yardbirds as he drank a bottle by himself.

Same bottle. Different day.

*To quote the great George Thorogood—I drink alone. WITH NOBODY ELSE!* screamed the murderer. His hands, still bleeding through the wrapped gauze from the earlier attack, were starting to throb. Apparently Peterson had given him more of a fight than he had originally expected. The fugitive's stomach was also quite sore, as the killer had forgotten to tape up Peterson's legs at first and was late to defend an unexpected kick from Peterson. But the murderer had already beaten Tommy so severely that the guitar legend wasn't going to escape anyway. If anything, Peterson's kick had only incensed the killer during the final minutes of the former rocker's life.

The murderer staggered over to the bathroom and swallowed a couple of painkillers to alleviate the pain. There wasn't a game plan for today, as the previous night's murder had taken its toll on him. One thing he wasn't worried about was a cop showing up at the door. The plan was executed flawlessly, with plenty of time to organize and analyze every detail before the attack took place. Even adding the small touches, such as placing various Stonehenge photographs around the studio, went right according to plan.

*Stonehenge.* Just the thought of that place began to enrage the murderer. The fact that some movie folks that created the fictional rockumentary *Spinal Tap* back in '83 could actually make money off jokes that poked fun of his 'concept' brought back sad memories.

For the killer, there was no joking about that place. He remembered the distant past as if it was yesterday: a supposed friend making some remarks connecting the ancient site to the murderer's band, one thing leading to another, and soon learning his band had become an 'inside joke' among some of the record executives. The wanted man was well aware that more often than not, an artist had one legitimate chance to launch a music career off into the right direction. Thousands upon thousands of bands knew that the window of opportunity opened and closed so fast so there was no room for error. And if the artistic vision wasn't clear, there were plenty of clueless music executives that would begin questioning your intentions. For the killer, that nightmare came true many, many years ago. It was impossible to go back in time.

Fumbling over to the dusty stereo, the murderer turned the volume up as the headphone jack was inserted. The black, twisted cord to his headphones was unusually long, running almost 50 feet in length. It gave the fugitive the ability to walk anywhere in the oversized room. The killer began untangling the cord as he walked towards his bay window. Leaning out, he watched two squirrels battle over an acorn as Black Sabbath's droaning song, 'Symptom of the Universe' rattled from the shaking headphones.

*Whose acorn is it?* he thought to himself. *Can they both share it or will one of them take the entire acorn for himself? And if one squirrel gets away with taking the entire acorn, how will the other squirrel react? Will he go right after the selfish squirrel or wait until the time is right and not only take back that acorn that they were supposed to share but make sure the other squirrel never ever gets the opportunity to take another acorn from anyone else?*

The killer's headphones began to slide off his head as he walked towards the basement door. It was time to decompress downstairs.

# CHAPTER 6

▼

A murderer was still on the loose in the unofficial capital in the world. And as Caitlin O'Connell entered the hotel minutes after leaving the Tommy Peterson crime scene, the detective was more than curious about meeting someone who may have been in contact with the deceased rocker shortly before he left last night's star-studded event.

With the media continuing to swarm around the lobby like bees on honey, O'Connell was already aware that Peterson had left the rock and roll bash early the previous night. But the networks kept broadcasting Peterson's acceptance speech every hour on the hour as if Peterson had been there all night.

O'Connell had gone over all the details from their security staff about Peterson's confrontation with an annoying fan before she arrived; the overzealous man had, as expected, already been accounted for when the murder took place. Hotel security, however, remembered one man in the company of Tommy Peterson last night that was here this morning.

The basic facts that O'Connell had so far was that Peterson was at the Waldorf-Astoria an hour before the show started, stayed backstage after picking up his plaque and left the hotel by himself. Peterson may have had contact with his killer but there was no way to tell for sure based on what she had heard so far. The preliminary police reports intimated that the murder scene smelled like someone had previous access to Peterson's studio loft, as there was no forced entry and no money taken from his wallet. That basic concept was steering O'Connell in one direction and one direction only. This murder was not looking like the work of a stranger or a crazed fan; the murderer and victim probably knew each other in some capacity. But it was now up to the detective to put all of the pieces together.

As O'Connell made her way over to the gentleman in question, she knew exactly whom the man was. The detective had recognized Tony Russo's face from a couple of rock documentaries on MTV and VH-1 specials. She also remembered his in-depth magazine interviews with some of the biggest names in rock and roll. O'Connell wasn't aware how close Russo was to Peterson, but the fact that he had just finished being interviewed by a TV reporter meant Russo was someone with information.

"Mr. Russo?" said O'Connell in her professional voice. "Tony Russo?"

"Yes?" said Russo. He knew right away she wasn't another irritating reporter. Her gold police badge was clearly visible.

"My name is Detective Caitlin O'Connell. I'm from homicide working on the Tommy Peterson murder case. Do you have a couple of minutes to talk to me, maybe over there?" She pointed to an area at the very far end of the lobby.

"Uh, yeah. I can talk," said Russo. The veteran reporter had his own questions to ask for his feature story but she had asked first.

"You know I recognized you from those TV music specials. I also used to read your articles in all those music magazines you used to write for," said O'Connell. "Good stuff."

"Oh really? Thanks. I'm still writing. I've been at this for a long, long time," replied Russo. Most people knew the rock personalities Russo was interviewing but hardly anyone knew who he was. He constantly had to show his invitation and ID to get into any stadium or backstage party. It was the rock journalist's curse: everyone in the band knew who Tony Russo was but that was usually it. He was happy to know that someone not in the music business like O'Connell knew who HE was for a change.

"You know I was totally into the rock scene in college," continued O'Connell. "I had a band myself and was a huge fan of The Winding Roads. Played all over the city clubs—you know, The Peppermint Lounge, The Mudd Club, and…"

"The others that no longer exist," said Russo. "So what happened?"

"Nothing—like what happened to basically all of the other bands like us in college. We had some decent songs but nothing great," sighed O'Connell.

Russo nodded his head in agreement but his mind today was elsewhere. "I'm sorry, detective. I'm having a tough time focusing right now on anything. I still can't believe Tommy's gone."

"I know what you mean," said O'Connell. "And how good of a friend?" Her pad was already out as she began to take notes.

"Well," replied Russo, "I knew Tommy when I first started out in the business, we hit it off after a couple of interviews, and we stayed friends ever since. I was working on helping him clean up his autobiography in between my writing gigs."

"So you knew him quite well then," said O'Connell. "Listen, I hate to cut this short, but I have to get to a couple of more musicians today before they leave New York. Can we talk a little later about Tommy? And you as well?"

Russo's demeanor went from sad to concerned. "Just so you know, detective, I was at…"

"Bowie's party last night. I know. We have an unofficial list of who was there, including you. I wouldn't ask you to help us if we thought you should be on the suspects list instead," replied O'Connell.

"That's good to know," said Russo. "But if you want my help, try to sound a bit sympathetic. Tommy was a good friend of mine."

"I'm sorry. You're absolutely right. I'll get in touch with you later." O'Connell handed Russo her business card. "Have you, uh, checked out yet?"

"No," said Russo. "I was going out for a walk when I first found out about Tommy."

"Good idea," said O'Connell. "Go get some air." She patted him on his shoulder and walked straight into the middle of the bustling lobby. Russo then buttoned up his jacket and headed outside onto Park Avenue. The television trucks were still lined up in front of the hotel, one right after the other. Walking west, Russo put his dark sunglasses on and stuck his hands inside his pockets.

*Murder*, thought Russo. *Who could have done such a thing?*

# CHAPTER 7

▼

As Detective O'Connell walked past one of the large conference rooms inside The Waldorf-Astoria, the faces walking past her were very familiar. One rock star after the other was milling about, comforting each other about the sad news of the late Tommy Peterson. But the most important face O'Connell spotted was none other than Peterson's longtime band mate and co-founding member of The Winding Roads—singer John Kenney. And it looked clear to her that he was getting prepped to make an announcement.

O'Connell remembered Kenney as a great counterpoint to Peterson. The guitarist Peterson was a mysterious intellectual of sorts while the singer Kenney was a friendly, rambunctious rebel—with both interchanging their roles as the leader of their band during their existence. O'Connell knew they had fought over money, band direction and their legacy like all of the other famous rock bands. But in the end, they always seemed to work it out. At least that's how it came off in the press. O'Connell moved her way through the crowd and reached out to tap Kenney on his shoulder.

"Yes?" the intense-looking Kenney said as he turned towards her.

For a second, O'Connell was a bit awestruck. The voice behind her favorite band was now speaking directly to her. But the detective soon realized why she was talking to Kenney in the first place and gained her composure.

"Mr. Kenney, I'm Detective Caitlin O'Connell from homicide. I need to talk with you briefly about…?"

"HOMICIDE?" said Kenney. "Oh, give me a break, sweetie! I'll talk to you when I'm ready. I've got to do this press thing first. Hey, who let this chick back here?"

The detective assumed Kenney thought he was back on tour and that a roadie from his massive entourage would take care of anyone interfering with the singer. O'Connell was also taken aback by his offensive demeanor, especially being referred to as a "chick." A wise person once told O'Connell "you should never meet your idols as you'll only be disappointed" and now she understood what that expression meant. Regardless of how much she liked The Winding Roads, the detective from Queens wasn't going to take any crap from anyone on a murder case she was working on.

"Mr. Kenney," barked O'Connell. "You listen and you listen good. I'll cuff you right now and take you downtown and you can do whatever it is you're doing here from a holding cell. You don't tell me what to do. I tell you." The room got quiet quickly as others in the vicinity started to drift away. Realizing his faux pas, Kenney reached out to shake her hand.

"You're right. I wasn't thinking. Give us a few minutes, folks." The singer walked into a small adjoining room away from the crowd as O'Connell followed behind. It was now just John Kenney and Caitlin O'Connell, alone in a room.

O'Connell was just three feet in front of the singer for The Winding Roads. At age 59, he looked in better shape than any other 59-year-old she knew. Kenney had his share of highs and lows but Peterson's murder was an extremely low point. Being a rock and roller for so many years meant that part of his success was simply surviving the insanity. Many of Kenney's rock friends died in the early, crazy days—like his one-time buddy Jim Morrison of The Doors—while others left the business when they reached middle age. But like Peterson, Kenney wasn't football coach or Boy Scout leader material. He was the singer for The Winding Roads, a big time rock and roller, and his behavior was often unpredictable.

"I have a short temper, you know, and I obviously wasn't listening. So I have no excuse," said the apologetic singer. "This hasn't been a great week in my life."

"That's ok," said O'Connell. "So you were not at the show last night with Peterson?"

"No. Tommy went alone," said Kenney. "That was the way we left it last week. I was at a party in Boston. I just got in here by private jet an hour or so ago."

"Would you mind telling me why you didn't go with him? It was an award for the band, not him, correct?" said O'Connell.

"Well, if you spoke to him every other day to him like I did for years, you would have thought it was an award for him anyway. And he didn't even want the stupid thing either!" Kenney then folded his arms.

"And that bothers you?" said O'Connell.

"No!" said Kenney. "What bothers me is not touring anymore. I mean Chuck Berry and Jerry Lee Lewis, our idols that were playing a decade before us, are still performing. And we're not! I mean The Stones are touring, The Dead is back. And where are we?"

"I'm not sure I'm following this," said a confused O'Connell. "Did you two have a fight?"

Kenney smiled. "I know where you're going with this. You don't get it, dear. Tommy and I have fought for years, decades, forever."

O'Connell interrupted. "I'm a fan of the band. I know your history."

"Right," said Kenney. "So you know we took all sort of swings at each other, threw bottles at each other, teed off on each other in the press. It's not uncommon, you know. Our UK friends Roger Daltrey and Pete Townshend of The Who have knocked heads for years. Or like those brothers, Liam and Noel Gallagher from Oasis, do now. When co-leaders of the band go at it, it's like a marriage that you really can never get out of. But Tommy wrote the stuff and was the creative force. So with awards like this one at the ceremony, it depends on what it is. Sometimes it's more or less who's around that wants to do it."

"I see," said O'Connell. "And what about the other guys in The Winding Roads? Have they been in touch with Tommy recently?"

"Nah," said Kenney. "Mike Going, our longtime keyboard man, has been beefing that Peterson didn't want to tour that much anymore so he got the Mike Going Band together to play the bills. Our drummer Andy Garger was pretty upset when his wife left him years ago and shacked up with Mike for a couple of years. But Andy's wife left Mike eventually and then Andy got remarried to an ex-girlfriend of mine. What can I say? It's a mess."

O'Connell once read a book about the infamous NYC godfathers of punk rock The Ramones and a story about band mates Joey and Johnny Ramone. Joey had a lifetime grudge over his mate Johnny (who were not related, as all band mates took the same surname) after marrying Joey's girlfriend. To their fans, they were united. To the two band mates, however, it was different. It was clear to the detective that The Winding Roads was looking less like a fun-loving band and more like a few guys working at a factory for years who had gotten tired of each other's company.

"I'd like to get some contact info about the other guys."

"Go right over there," said Kenney as he pointed to Bob Wittman, their long-time manager. "He'll give you whatever you need."

"Thanks," said O'Connell. "And John, I know this is sort of, uh, a strange request, but would you mind if I got a photo with you?" The detective couldn't believe what she had just said. She was investigating the Tommy Peterson murder case but she had always wanted a photo with John Kenney.

"Sure. Interrogate me on the spot and then ask me for a photo op. This is what my life is like!" said the smirking Kenney. "But I know you're trying to get to the bottom of this case, so I'll put you in a different category. Hey Bob, over here! This detective wants a photo."

Kenney's manager Bob Wittman, clearly not amused by the prying detective's request, took the disposable camera from her and snapped a quick photo of O'Connell and Kenney arm in arm. The star-struck detective knew her chief would flip out if he saw this picture, so O'Connell was happy it was taken out of view from the nearby media people.

"Now go out and get that bastard!" barked Kenney. "And after you do, I want a few minutes alone with that dirt bag."

"We'll take care of what needs to be done. We'll be in touch," replied O'Connell.

She wasn't sure why Kenney felt the need to fly down to New York City so soon but as the voice of The Winding Roads, her assumption was that the singer assumed he would be forced here anyway to address all of the police and media requests. Kenney also knew the funeral services were right around the corner and he wanted to be involved in the planning. It was the least Kenney could do for his lifetime musical partner.

O'Connell tucked her small camera away and took out her cell phone as Kenney headed back towards the growing crowd of media people. She had changed her mind about leaving the hotel; it was time to dial up Tony Russo again. If this rock reporter friend of Peterson's was working on his autobiography, O'Connell concluded *he* was the person with the detailed knowledge about Tommy Peterson's life, someone that could direct her to nabbing the fugitive. The whole thing sounded a bit unconventional, but the detective needed a 'silent partner' on the case. And Russo's reporter background skills fit the description to a tee.

# CHAPTER 8

▼

The Manhattan sky was getting dark as it started to drizzle and Tony Russo was without an umbrella as he walked through the midtown streets. After the horrible World Trade Center attacks of September 11th, you no longer could stroll through adjoining office buildings in the Big Apple to duck out of the rain. The government officials decided that a terrorist attack could come in many different forms, and losing 2,749 lives in one day wasn't going to happen again. The casual building walk-throughs were a thing of the past.

But Russo continued west anyway towards 48th Street and Broadway where the legendary music store, Manny's, was open for business. Russo's kids had their favorite toy store where they wanted to play with every toy they could get their hands on. Manny's was Russo's version of the toy store.

The first item that caught Russo's eye as he entered was a brown Gibson SG double neck guitar. It was only a matter of seconds before he was pretending to be Jimmy Page while avoiding the opening chords to Led Zeppelin's 'Stairway To

Heaven' to the delight of the shell-shocked salespeople. Wandering into the keyboard section, he played a few measures of 'Comfortably Numb' by Pink Floyd while using every different tone setting that the Yamaha P120 on display had available. Russo even sat behind a new Roland TD-6S V-Tour electronic drum kit. With the sound of the drums coming only through his headphones, Russo could bash away forever on the kit without bothering a living soul.

But none of this was able to shake Russo's depression. As he headed out of Manny's, the veteran rock writer found Tommy Peterson's picture way up on the wall, standing onstage with his trademark guitar: a vintage Vox Mark VI ivory white, egg-shaped guitar made in Italy. He had seen that photo up there a million times before but it seemed different now. Instead of looking like a photo seen in a rock history book, it only reminded Russo of something he might have caught in a newspaper's obituary section.

As Russo turned back east to the hotel, he continued to reminisce about how Tommy's friendship had changed his life. He was not a family member, band mate or an old neighborhood friend that Peterson had grown up with. But the fact that the two became close gave Russo instant credibility among his peers early on in his career. And Peterson's associations with well-known politicians, movie stars, technology billionaires, European royalty and other high-profile personalities enabled Russo to converse with people he never would have met on his own.

Taking the elevator back up to his room, Russo packed up the rest of his belongings in a hurry and ran down the hall to catch the closing elevator doors. He wanted to get the first cab available to Penn Station and then any train out of the Long Island Rail Road station—even if it meant waiting at the Jamaica transfer stop for a connecting train. The detective would have to come out and visit Russo at his place if it was that important. Just as the elevator reached the lobby floor, Russo's cell phone rang.

"Hello?" said Russo.

"Tony. It's Detective O'Connell. Where are you right now?"

As the doors opened, Russo could see the detective standing by the hotel checkout desk. He knew that O'Connell had already inquired if the rock journalist had left the hotel. Before Russo could answer the detective's question, she spotted him standing inside the elevator. O'Connell closed her cell phone and walked towards the reporter. Russo had nowhere to go.

"I'm right here," said Russo with a fake smile.

O'Connell smiled back as they met face to face once again. "Well hello again, Tony. Understand you're checking out today. But as you know, there is a time element involved here. So the way I see it, you seem like a logical person for me to start with. I know you probably didn't have much of a breakfast, so can we grab an early lunch and talk at length about Tommy Peterson?"

Russo was disappointed he couldn't get out of the hotel in time and now he was stuck with a pushy detective. The NYPD was apparently one step ahead of him. "I guess so," said Russo. "Let me check out of here and you pick the place."

"Deal," said O'Connell as Russo proceeded to the front desk to settle his bill. He began to think of a number of places where they could go to get this over and done with. But judging from the look on O'Connell's face, Russo believed that the detective already had someplace in mind.

"So where are we headed off to?" asked Russo as he tucked his hotel bill away in his bag.

"The Hard Rock Café. A perfect place to jog your memory while we talk," said O'Connell.

Russo furrowed his brow. "Really? You think a crowded, theme-based restaurant is the kind of place for me to gather my thoughts?" replied Russo. "But you're paying, so if that's what you think, let's get there before the crowds come in."

"I know, I know. It's 10:35 and it opens at 11. They'll take us right away with my badge," responded O'Connell as they walked towards the hotel exit. "Follow me out this way."

Russo grabbed his bags as he followed the detective out to the street and into the unmarked police car. The second Russo closed the door, O'Connell floored the car and bolted across town with her red light and siren wailing. Russo immediately snapped on his seatbelt. He thought the whole siren thing seemed a bit dramatic just to have lunch but Russo was not about to tell O'Connell how to drive.

"So do you have any ideas as to who might have murdered Tommy?" said O'Connell as she turned sharply down another street.

Russo was holding on to the dashboard for dear life. He had once been on the back of Vince Neil's motorcycle, the hell-raising singer for the Eighties metal band Mötley Crüe. That experience alone was enough to last the rock critic a lifetime. "No I don't!" answered Russo. "And why are you driving so fast?"

O'Connell chuckled. "Oh, it's not that fast. You should see me when I'm in a rush." The detective negotiated another sharp turn while jumping the curb. "So no one comes to mind at all?"

Russo said, "I really haven't thought about it much. I guess I've been thinking more about Tommy and his family."

"Understood," replied O'Connell. "But the longer we don't think about who the possibilities might be, the more time we're giving this maniac an opportunity to vanish from our radar screen."

"Okay," said Russo. "So tell me…"

The police car suddenly came to an abrupt halt as O'Connell slammed on the brakes, sending Russo and all of his things onto the dirty floor of the police car.

"Why did you stop like that?" yelled Russo. "We're going to lunch, not the emergency room!"

"I know that!" replied O'Connell. "Sorry about that quick stop. Don't forget to grab your stuff."

As Russo stepped onto the sidewalk, he tilted his head straight up to see the back end of the 1957 Chevy Thunderbird sticking out from above the Hard Rock sign. He felt the detective was already pushing the envelope as to how much information she was demanding. But Russo assumed this was the way detectives worked. After O'Connell showed her police badge at the door, the two were let into the well-known eatery before the doors had opened to the entire public. The detective pointed to one specific corner table.

"We need to grab that corner booth right over there," said O'Connell to the surprised manager. "It's police business."

The manager took two menus from a busy waiter. "Ok. But detective, I need to ask. Is there a problem here that we should know about?"

"Nope," said O'Connell. "We're conducting some research on a case and that's all I can tell you. But it has absolutely nothing to do with your restaurant. So there's nothing for you to worry about."

The manager was visibly relieved. "Thank God. I was beginning to wonder. Let me know if we can help with anything else."

O'Connell sat down at a booth with Russo that had an interesting display box sticking out from the wall.

"See that, Tony?"

Russo took a closer look at a faded orchestral score with lots of words scribbled in between the staff lines. "What is this?"

O'Connell pointed to the plaque below the display box that was affixed to the wall. It read:

*Orchestral Score of the 'Everything Is Nothing' Album*

*From the 1992 Rockin' Symphony Express Tour*

*Donated by Tommy Peterson of The Winding Roads*

Russo remembered that Peterson once gave the rights out to an entertainment group that put together a symphony tour that played dramatic orchestrated music versions of well-known rock songs. It was a small success but Peterson never went to see his masterpiece performed in this setting. For his rocker buddy Tommy, it was more about getting the money fronted to him during a cash shortage.

"I see you've been here before, detective. You know, Tommy told me recently that every few years, there was always one rock song every new teenage guitar player needed to learn from the decade before," said Russo. "In the Sixties, you had to know 'Johnny B Goode.' The Seventies was 'Twist And Shout.' The Eighties? 'Smoke On The Water.' And The Nineties, it was 'I

Will Follow.' And right now, I know every kid in a music store knows how to jam to 'Smells Like Teen Spirit.' Not the leads but the songs. Tommy said it didn't matter if you liked the band or the artist; some songs you just had to know, especially if you were hoping to find others to jam with."

Russo turned his head to the display. "But this orchestra thing you're pointing to? It wasn't like Tommy hated it but the essence of what made rock songs great was kind of lost with this symphony thing. Then again, Tommy said he got paid well off the deal. He gave up figuring out what the fans liked or not after his first solo record."

"See? I thought sitting here might get you thinking," said O'Connell. The detective took out a legal pad and pen and cleared the food from the space in front of her. "So let's start from the beginning. I know a lot about this band but you know the specifics, the meat and potatoes. What I need most from you is names and timeframes and why they might be important as we move along in the case."

"I see," said Russo. "But Tommy worked with a ton of people. I don't think you have any idea of how long this will take. Plus, you're looking for someone who obviously didn't like him. That may be an endless list."

"I know what I'm up against. But you know his story almost as well as Tommy, maybe better since you're a step away from what happened. Again, let's just start from the beginning," said O'Connell.

Russo laughed. "Ha! I'm the reporter on a deadline trying to do a story on Tommy. You know I should be asking you the questions, not the other way around."

"Tony, let's not do this downtown in a room with a giant white light dangling over your head?" O'Connell had a weird grin on her face.

Russo rubbed his chin as he stared back at Peterson's scribbles inside the framed display. This was easily going to be a three-hour lunch.

# CHAPTER 9

▼

At the very end of the last aisle in Tower Records, the murderer was fumbling around with the headphones by one of their standalone jukeboxes. He didn't want to stay home and thought it was best to get out and clear his head. The killer wanted to prove to himself that he was fine and there were better days ahead, now that Tommy Peterson had been disposed of.

Even though the store had only a handful of people inside during the mid-morning hours, the music retailer always gave their potential customers the opportunity to listen to the latest CDs. An interesting conversation between a father and son caught the killer's attention. He saw the older man hand his son a CD while saying "if you want to learn how to write a rock song, you have to go back and listen to *Abbey Road* by these guys. The Beatles!" to which the son replied, "Oh yeah, that's the Paul McCartney guy. He was in that band Wings, right? Was that his first band?" The father walked away from the aisle disgusted as his son laughed while putting his Apple iPod earpiece back in. The young man was going back, all the way back to 1989 to Nirvana's first release *Bleach*. That was far enough for the teenager.

The wanted man smirked and kept on browsing. Most of the retail music stores, who were fighting a battle with the global online digital downloading world, were hoping a music sample or two would lead to the possibility of a CD purchase. However, the fugitive was not interested in buying anything on today's music charts. He was in search of an old single of his own possibly deep within the discount CD bins.

As he lowered his body further into one particular bin, he spotted a familiar Sixties band's name: The Sticky Buns. His old friend Susan Decker's band. The Buns had been thrown onto this Sixties compilation CD as the second-to-last track out of 21. *Wow, what an honor. To be sandwiched in between The Martonians and The Blue Dalmatians,* commented the murderer. *No wonder they never made it either.*

The search for the single was an unsuccessful one. Besides, the wanted man didn't like compilation CDs, even though it was better to be on a CD than not. The killer peeked at the price of the CD, which depressed him even more. It was on sale for $5.99, which was roughly two-thirds less than what the new CDs were selling for. But it was a basic supply and demand situation. The murderer didn't own the rights to the songs anyway, so what was the point of even looking?

The murderer took the CDs he had pulled out and threw them right back into the bin as ventured over towards the books section. On display were dozens of music biographies on many of the past and present music superstars—Elvis, Eric Clapton, U2, Madonna, Metallica—as well as several quirky books that seemed less exciting. One colorful oversized book was all about how fashion and rock music blended together—the overcoat mods and The Small Faces, the shiny glam kids and Marc Bolan, the safety-pinned punks and The Sex Pistols, the big-haired ladies and Poison, the flannel slackers and Pearl Jam. *Useless books with useless information*, muttered the killer. *It's only about the music.*

Working his way down the display table, he discovered a familiar book that the killer had not seen in ages:

### *Speeding On The Rock and Roll Highway:*

### The Story of The Winding Roads

The murderer began to mumble a bit louder, saying things like *No more speeding for you, Tommy boy. You're out of gas.* The killer opened up the biography and began to thumb through the glossy pages. He noticed that the authors were apparently demented Winding Roads fans, who had everything but the kitchen sink displayed in the book: rare home photos, worn ticket stubs, faded contracts, handwritten notes, detailed interviews, annotations and lists. The size of the book alone could make one wonder if the band even remembered all that had happened to them over the course of their career.

Towards the middle of the retrospective book, the murderer's eyes locked on to a photo that was taken outside a club—it was Tommy Peterson standing next to the killer himself. The caption wasn't as important as the date of the photo:

### *Summer 1968*

*Yeah,* the fugitive said to himself. *Buddies forever. But I know what you did, Tommy. You think you were that clever and that I had no idea of what was going on? You were so wrapped up in yourself you couldn't even think clearly, let alone do what you did by yourself. You were as out of control as the rest of us back then, but at least I had the decency to be honest. Instead, you were as shifty as the first day I met you on the studio set at the BBC. Suspicious and paranoid is what you always were. And thanks again for managing to transfer all your negative forces over to me.*

As the killer rambled on about the photo he was staring at, his right hand that had been holding the page was now ripping the page down and through the middle. The internal rage that was lodged inside of him was now being redirected onto the photo he was staring at. It was another sign that proved the killer's hatred for Tommy Peterson had not waned at all.

Unknown to the psychotic musician was the music store's manager, who was carefully watching this disturbed individual wrecking the store's merchandise. Music stores always had their share of oddballs but they tended to be under the age of 30 and 'under the influence' of something. Even the head clerk hadn't seen the "customer" come in. To both employees, however, this guy was nothing but another pain in the neck that was damaging the goods. The clerk decided to put a stop to the customer's behavior.

"Excuse me," said the clerk, "but are you planning on buying that book, because…"

The murderer stopped ripping the page and turned slowly towards the clerk. Being interrupted was something that didn't fly well with unpredictable, angry artist types.

"Blah blah blah," said the fugitive.

The clerk, barely 17 and half the height and weight of the customer, took a step back at the scary look the killer gave him. For the lousy minimum wage he was making, it wasn't worth taking on an agitated stranger. But the clerk wanted one more shot at him.

"Hey, if you're not going to buy that book, then I'm going to have to ask you to leave," said the nervous clerk.

The killer slowly closed the book and then spit on the cover, leaving a long trail of saliva dangling from his lips. "Fine," he said, "but ask me nicely. I'm all ears, friend. And you'll have to come closer because I don't hear too well from over here."

The clerk slowly retreated from the older man. Something was definitely not right with this person but it wasn't worth figuring out what that agenda was. It was time to get the cops involved.

"Renee, call the cops!" yelled the clerk as he darted down the aisle and away from the oddball customer.

"How DARE you say such a thing!" said the killer as he headed down the aisle towards the clerk. "I haven't committed a crime. The fact that you don't even know who I am proves to me you're nothing but a worthless bug."

"You stay away from me! STAY AWAY!" screamed the fleeing clerk.

A few of the other shoppers in the store were carefully watching what was transpiring towards the front of the record store. Of course, there were no undercover cops or Good Samaritans today. It was just a bunch of puzzled teenagers. The murderer was approaching the counter when the store manager was holding the phone and getting ready to dial.

"I'd put that down, sweetheart," said the murderer. "That could be dangerous."

"Please don't do anything to me," said the nervous woman. As the killer turned around, he saw two teenagers talking on cell phones in the back that were staring at him. It was obvious to the killer that the police would be here in a couple of minutes. He yelled over to them:

"I KNOW WHAT YOU'RE DOING. DON'T COME BACK HERE BECAUSE I KNOW WHAT YOU LOOK LIKE. I NEVER FORGET THOSE WHO HAVE DONE ME WRONG!"

The teenagers, standing in different parts of the store, folded up their cell phones and retreated near the back of the store. The murderer smiled and turned back to the front door. The question for him now was simple. How fast could he get out of here?

"Lock the door behind me and then run to the back to the store," said the killer to the store manager.

The woman did as she was told and then scampered out of sight. The killer had parked only a short distance away from the store. Since no one in the mini-mall knew what had happened inside, the murderer strolled through the parking lot and drove away without incident. There wasn't a police or mall security car to be heard as his 1973 red Impala turned onto Franklin Avenue. Once again, he had beaten the odds.

*If I knew evading the police was this easy, I would have settled a lot more scores that way, dear old Tommy*, thought the fugitive. As a child, the killer had always been fascinated by how mobsters got away with committing tons of crimes without getting caught. As the killer daydreamed of missed opportunities and dishonest people he had encountered in his brief musical career, he was unaware he was in the middle of another meltdown. The speed of his mind was now pushing the speed of his car far beyond the 30 mph speed limit.

Out of nowhere, a family of four was crossing the intersection as the murderer began to drive through the solid red light that was showing. The prime suspect, seeing the family at the last second, slammed on the brakes, spinning his car in a 360-degree circle as the terrified family scampered back to the sidewalk to safety. Covered in sweat, the murderer sat quietly in the car for a few seconds, refusing to acknowledge the screaming father of the family outside his window. He then floored the car away from the father and down a side street, disappearing from sight.

The old-school rocker had discovered the hard way that he was not ready to start walking around the stores and streets as if nothing had happened the past 36 hours. Besides, there was more to be done. It was just a matter of focusing on the 'when' and 'how'. The killer already knew *why*.

# CHAPTER 10

▼

Both Russo and O'Connell looked over the menu in front of the waiter. Although the detective was ready to order, Russo wasn't very hungry. Cops were used to eating at unscheduled times, but this journalist always ate at 1pm. Even when the routinely tardy rock bands kept Russo waiting, he had a sandwich and drink in his bag. The fact that Russo was being recruited as a source of information led him to believe he was now indirectly involved in a manhunt for Tommy Peterson's killer. The reality of that situation only contributed to Russo's lack of appetite.

"I'll think I'll just have some soup and a glass of water," said Russo.

O'Connell said, "Tony, I'm ordering a cheeseburger with everything on it. As long as that gives you enough energy to help me get some quality Tommy Peterson information, I don't care what you eat."

Russo made a face at the detective. "You know I don't even have to be here. I've got work I have to get back to soon."

"I know your magazine is planning to do a special feature on this case in the magazine you're working for. But we'll find a way to make it work for both of us."

Russo shook his head in disgust. All he could see was Johnny Merseburg with his production and marketing team laying out the special issue on Tommy Peterson and The Winding Roads without him. His publisher was expecting big things from Russo as an insider to a murder case that doubled as a great rock and roll story. But he hadn't written a single word yet.

"Well, thanks. That puts things in perspective," said Russo.

"We all have bosses we have to report to, so the faster you help me, the faster you can get back to your job," replied a smirking O'Connell.

Over the years, Russo had watched some of the most vile, untalented dregs of humanity become rock superstars and make millions of dollars because they had become "the next big thing." But although rock journalists were part of the success for many artists, they were neither part of the band nor their management. Russo got paid for the story he wrote and that was the end of it. Wall Street journalists sometimes got lucrative advice from analysts or bankers. War correspondents won Pulitzer Prizes and television gigs. Rock journalists just had to be satisfied writing about rock and roll music and not much else. There was no "cashing in" for Russo.

"So let's get on with this, shall we?" said Russo. "What do you want to know and how can I help?"

As the waiter took back their menus, O'Connell took a sip from her beer. "Well, I know a lot about Tommy Peterson as a fan of his music. And I know a little about his personality from the papers and interviews. But you KNOW him. This autobiography you were assisting him with may have something in there that will reveal who we're looking for. It's not a sure bet, mind you, but I think it's a good place to start. So what we need to do is to construct a list of his family members, close friends, band mates and people related to The Winding Roads. We should also make a list of those he has had problems with in the past and present. The two lists might have the same names on it, so after we compile the list we'll analyze it."

"I hope you have a lot of ink in that pen," said Russo. "This is a guy that has entertained for over 40 years and has been involved with thousands of people and projects."

"It doesn't matter if it's a million," replied O'Connell. "We have to start somewhere. Hopefully we'll be able to eliminate some of them as we continue to reexamine the crime scene evidence. So let's start with those people closest to Peterson and work our way down from the list."

O'Connell took out a giant yellow pad and a black magic marker and wrote at the top in caps:

### TOMMY PETERSON F&F

"F&F?" asked Russo.

"Friends And Family," replied O'Connell. "I could have written 'Suspects' but that would be a bit presumptuous, right?"

Russo said nothing as he stared down at the blank page. Instead of finishing an outline of Peterson's life with Tommy, he was now creating a different outline of Peterson's life with a stranger in order to find his killer. Their friendship had now put him in a unique situation. If Russo started helping with the investigation, people close to Peterson would have to be contacted. He knew several folks would not enjoy the inquiries, especially those who had past run-ins with the rocker. If Russo decided not to help with the case and word got out, perhaps those in the music biz who wanted justice would end their own relationship with Russo. It was a no-win situation.

"Whatever. Let's get this over with. I'll start from the beginning and run through his life quickly and then we can circle back. Let me take my notes out." Russo took out a rolled-up stack of paper, some of which he had used in organizing Peterson's book.

"Can I see that?" said a startled O'Connell.

"It's all in shorthand and abbreviations and my own code. I write this way so no one but me can read it," said Russo.

"Fine by me. So give me what you've got, starting back when Tommy first got into music."

Russo took a deep breath. "In 1963, Tommy was in high school and hated it. He had fallen in love with rock and roll and was desperate to find a band to play his songs. He knew drummer Andy Garger and keyboardist Mike Going from class. The three met singer John Kenney and bassist Steve Mars at a party. The band took off rather fast as the chemistry worked. So Peterson and the rest of them were done with school."

"Done?" asked O'Connell.

"Done. Soon they were playing all over Manhattan and caught the eye of Ryan Guttridge and Joe Acevedo, these two music managers, and the next thing they knew they had them signed to MetroSound Records. By around '67, The Winding Roads were operating at full steam, especially Peterson. He had written three relatively successful albums for the band, married a hot babe in photographer Mary Pat O'Callaghan, and became a father to his kids Colleen and Dylan."

"So Tommy was moving rather fast," interrupted O'Connell.

"If you were a successful Wall Street guy, that pace would be par for the course," replied Russo. "But in a fast-paced world of rock and roll, it was hard to be on tour, write hit records and keep up with everything like trying to be a family man. It was a lot of pressure that hit Peterson quick and the band wasn't making things any easier on him."

"How so?" said O'Connell.

"Well, after the *Everything Is Nothing* record became a mega-selling hit in '69, the band had got deeper into the excesses of the rock and roll life: women, drugs, spending money, you name it. They certainly weren't alone in the late Sixties. Many bands coming out of the Woodstock generation were out of control. And the band wanted to do more and more touring. But Tommy hated the road. In particular, he hated the constant invasion of privacy, especially after some guy broke into their apartment and tied his family up."

"I remember reading about that," said O'Connell.

"Yeah, and that was back in the early days. But I think his wife Mary Pat never got over the intrusions. She later split with the kids as that next tour got started. She knew the groupies were always surrounding her hubby but the home invasion thing freaked her out. And since Tommy didn't know how to deal with it, he just threw himself into the next record and tour and kept going. By '74, the band was a mess and their bassist Steve Mars was asked to leave the band as he was strung out. When they found him dead a month later, my competitors had a field day with Tommy. They said instead of helping Mars, some said Peterson simply ignored Mars. And that wasn't the case at all. Mars said to Tommy that he wanted to write his own songs and was sick of Peterson calling all the shots. But Peterson was still devastated by Steve's death."

"How did Tommy respond?" said O'Connell.

"Tommy threw himself into a flurry of writing over the next year, putting out his first solo CD and writing another record for The Roads. But the music scene was starting to change as the punks and new wavers zipped by them in the late Seventies. And by the time he started working on *Moonshine* in '80, John Lennon of the Beatles and John Bonham of Led Zeppelin, two of Tommy's favorite rockers, had died. When the record finally came out, MTV was off and running. It was the beginning of the end. The Winding Roads supported the record but there was no video to go with it and the record fell off the charts. Peterson was done. He just wasn't motivated."

"So things got better for him after he left the band?" inquired O'Connell.

"Well, not exactly," replied Russo. "Once you leave a band with a giant imprint like The Winding Roads, the fans don't have to follow you. And if they don't, the label isn't jumping through hoops for an older artist. If you look at many older rockers who moved on from their well-known band, they tend to drift off into unknown musical territory only to return to the past. I know guys like Robert Plant of Led Zeppelin probably likes his solo life more now than before but some Zep fans have a hard time buying his new stuff, which, by the way, is quite cool. Tommy would get together on very rare occasions with his old band but not much. Tommy had enough money coming in from the royalties so he didn't feel obligated to revisit the past. At first."

"Ah, so there were some money issues there."

"Well, he enjoyed the first three or four years away from The Roads but Tommy was having trouble drawing people to his solo career. Then he got involved in a couple of business ventures that were probably not a good idea and by the beginning of the Nineties, he was second-guessing what he wanted to do with the remainder of his career. And the money infusion from the Roads reunions did help."

"A familiar story," said O'Connell. "So what I think we need to do here is identify the most well-known Peterson situations that might have affected somebody in a negative way."

Russo stared out across the restaurant. "Then we need to focus on three areas: the artistic, meaning someone getting screwed out of something Tommy did musically; the business, meaning someone got ripped off money-wise by Tommy; or the relationship, you know, someone getting close to Peterson that got hurt. That's how I see it."

O'Connell took out a fresh piece of paper and drew three lines down the pad for four columns—ART, BIZ, LOVE—with a far left column to be used for names. As O'Connell looked up at Russo waiting for a response, he started to run through as many names as he possibly could.

"John Kenney, check him down for ART and BIZ. Guttridge and Acevedo, BIZ. Indigo, LOVE. No, wait. Make her all three."

"Indigo?" inquired O'Connell.

"His longtime girlfriend. And Caitlin, don't interrupt me. If you want me to do this right, let me blast out as many names as

I can think of and I'll explain why they are in one, two or all three of the columns," said Russo.

"I'll keep my mouth shut." O'Connell was aware that even with all the names Russo was about to give her, there was a reasonable expectation that the killer might not be on this list. Although she was hoping to eliminate others and focus on others in the process, there was a risk of going this route. Without pausing, Russo began naming names to the detective, one after the other, knowing that O'Connell had no idea just how many names he was about to give her today.

# CHAPTER 11

▼

As Caitlin O'Connell rubbed her writing hand, she was impressed with the results. Looking over a couple of hundred rock and roll and entertainment-related names over a span of four decades, Tony Russo said he would deliver as many names as he could think of related to Tommy Peterson and The Winding Roads. And he came through with flying colors.

"Cool list, huh? The top and the bottom in music, high society, politics, you name it. I hope this is going to help you, even though I don't see how," said Russo.

O'Connell scanned the pages she had spread out across the table. There was a ton of leads to work from this list. "Tony, this is right on the money. I think this is a start in the right direction. What we have to...."

But before the detective could finish her sentence, Russo's cell phone rang. He recognized the number all too well. It was his boss, Johnny Merseburg. Russo knew he had to take this call. He couldn't imagine how angry his boss might be at this point in time but he was now about to find out.

"Hold that thought," said Russo.

"Go ahead. I want to start making some notes here on the side," said O'Connell.

Russo slowly opened his cell phone to take the call. "Hey, Johnny. Sorry I…"

Merseburg cut him off immediately. "Tony, you better get your butt in here in 15 minutes. Your wife said you're in Manhattan? Where are you? Are you still trolling around with that cop?" It was clear his boss had no time for idle chitchat.

"Yeah. But I…"

Merseburg stopped the veteran reporter off again in mid-sentence. "Didn't she get what she needed already? You know I pay your salary, your health benefits, and your expenses! Remember that part? 'Cause the NYPD does NOT!"

Russo had no answers to his angry publisher's questions. Johnny Merseburg had given him an assignment and he had failed. Not at getting close to the right sources or doing the research needed for the Peterson story but getting the actual story written and submitted on time. Russo was supposed to be a professional journalist but he wasn't acting like one and Merseburg was calling him on it. The friendship he had developed with Tommy Peterson was affecting Russo from doing his job.

"Sorry," said Russo.

"No. Sorry doesn't cut it this time," said Merseburg. "Tony, you're not some clueless college grad on his first big story. You're an old pro, you have a job and I want it done and want it done now. So wrap up whatever it is you're doing there with the police, get all your notes together and get your butt down here. I need something on this story. NOW!" The line went dead.

Merseburg was right. It was time the seasoned rock writer started doing what he was getting paid to do—write the big Tommy Peterson cover story for the rock and roll magazine he was working for. Russo folded the cell phone cover down and turned to O'Connell.

"Detective..." said Russo.

"Caitlin," the detective replied.

"Caitlin, I have to go back to work and get this story done," said Russo. "Unless you feel like paying my salary, I need to save my job. But listen, I'm pretty sure that there are a couple of books in the bookstores available on The Winding Roads. Just use the index in the back of those books to cross-reference some of the names I gave you. But I gotta get out of here."

"I will," said O'Connell. "And Tony, remember that this is an ongoing investigation so be very careful about what you're writing about and who you talk to. I'll keep reminding you. And I'll see you at the wake tomorrow and the Peterson memorial concert Sunday night. I will call you later."

With all that was going on, Russo had forgotten about the concert—something else that he'd now have to find time for. He slid all of his stuff off the table and into his bag and exited out of the Hard Rock Café. It was bad enough he had to attend the concert but now he was on call with both work and the police department. His wife was not going to be happy.

"Bye bye," said O'Connell.

Russo waved his hand up in the air. Out on the street, like a miracle, a taxicab appeared out of nowhere. Jumping into the sedan, he told the cabbie to head south to 23$^{rd}$ Street as fast as he could.

Since Russo had nothing typed out yet—most of the narrative was stuck inside his head—he tried to visualize what was happening over at the magazine he worked. Assuming Merseburg's competent staff was already creating and collating all sorts of sidebars, photo layouts and extended quotes from other well-known rockers, the upcoming issue was in good shape. But as the ghostwriter for Peterson's unpublished autobiography, his publisher's expectation for a 'special' story from a close friend of Tommy Peterson's was evident. Russo had the potential to make a decent story great, and they were all banking on that at *Rock Forever*.

The cab had made remarkable time and pulled up in front of Russo's building in just a few minutes. Throwing the cab driver money and not waiting for a receipt, he rushed into the building and took the elevator up to the twenty-sixth floor. As Russo entered the offices of *Rock Forever,* he tried to gain his composure in the upscale atmosphere his boss had created. This entertainment magazine operated better than most magazines; Russo actually had an office with a door after years of working in dingy cubicles. Merseburg also paid his workers 20% better than the competition. With a seemingly endless stream of cash, the publisher refused to walk into anything less than an attractive environment every day.

As Russo walked towards Merseburg's office, everyone was avoiding eye contact with him. He knew that was a bad sign but there was nothing he could do about it now. Russo's walk slowed as he approached the corner office, coming to a dead halt just a few feet from the entrance. He tucked in his shirt, pulled up his pants and walked through the open door.

"Well, well, Detective Russo. Do we have a break in the case yet? HAVE YOU FORGOTTEN WE GO TO PRESS IN TWO DAYS?" yelled the agitated Merseburg. His boss, standing in the middle of his office with papers at his feet, looked as if he hadn't slept in a couple of days.

"Johnny," exclaimed Russo, "Listen, I had no choice. She was stalking me in the lobby, calling me on the phone, making me go to lunch. It's a murder investigation so what do you want from me? Tell the cops that I won't help them? They don't like that very much."

"Alright, alright," said Merseburg. "I got the point. Sit down over there."

Russo sat down on the oversized couch as Merseburg pulled up a chair in front of him. He hated sitting there only because the cushions were not firm and anyone weighing more than 180 pounds would sink deep into his couch. Russo was convinced he kept the old couch because Merseburg enjoyed trapping his difficult employees.

"Tony, I need copy and fast and you're my insider," said Merseburg. "But how are we supposed to talk about what you're doing when you're off running around with the cops?"

"I know, I know. I think that…"

Merseburg continued. "We have the opportunity to create a very unique piece: a mega-obituary! I want copy on the first time you guys met, I want stories that no one else has heard, I want new interview stuff from his ex-pals, and I want something on that autobiography Peterson was trying to get off the ground."

Russo squirmed in the couch as he tried to get a quick word or two past his hyperventilating boss. "Tommy's book? Yes. There's a ton of info I have access to."

Merseburg nodded his head. "Well, there you go! You know, the other day I read excerpts from Bob Dylan's autobiography and it was great. What you need to do is give us some insights as to what Tommy was writing about and how far he got. It's very simple, no?"

"Well, I wouldn't say simple," quipped Russo. "It's not like I've been throwing pencils in the ceiling."

Merseburg got up from his chair and pointed his finger at Russo. "Don't get smart with me, Tony. We've got great photos and sidebars waiting for this freaking story. The hole on the galleys, where your story should be, will be directly proportional to the hole in your checking account if you don't get that story in soon. And don't forget to be at that memorial concert as well. We'll need a story on all that too."

"Anything else?" said Russo.

"Just find your office, find your notes, find your computer and do the story. I'm done talking." Merseburg left his office without waiting for a response from the weary journalist. His boss didn't even seem to care that he had lost a close friend in Tommy Peterson. Merseburg was all about getting the story.

Sitting in his boss' couch for a minute, Russo gathered his thoughts for a moment. He knew the best rock stories were always those that came from writers who had not only broken into the inner circle of a well-known artist but had been part of their life. Although Russo was still upset from Peterson's untimely death, he knew he would have to find a way to write something insightful without disrespecting Peterson's legacy and, of course, without revealing anything from his conversations with Detective O'Connell.

Russo pulled himself up from the couch and left Merseburg's office. As he walked into his office, instead of sitting down at the desk, Russo stood up on the radiator against the window and stared down at the busy streets below. The hardest part was figuring out how to start. If his article started off too flowery, the readers might think Russo was making this notoriously difficult rocker into some sort of saint. If the piece began sounding too factual, others would think a bunch of editorial assistants were ghost writing it and the magic would be noticeably absent.

*Stop thinking so much*, thought Russo, *and just start typing.*

# CHAPTER 12

▼

Standing in the Lawrence Krugman funeral home parking lot, Detective O'Connell looked at her watch while a light rain continued to fall. It was 8:30 pm and Tony Russo was late. This place was in his neck of the woods—suburban Nassau County—so she knew he wouldn't miss Tommy Peterson's private wake service. But O'Connell had already spent a great deal of time with Russo and knew he had a story to file at his magazine. However, she was hoping her "detective apprentice" would show up soon.

Although Peterson had spent almost his entire adult career in New York City, his mother, Eileen, had lived for years in an apartment complex on Long Island. She decided that there would definitely be a Roman Catholic wake and funeral. Overhearing Peterson's mother, O'Connell learned that Eileen wasn't waiting for that "annoying ex-wife of his" Mary Pat to make a decision and his "floozy girlfriend" Indigo had no legal claim to Peterson's final resting place. Apparently the deceased rocker never made out a will, which was no surprise to anyone.

But O'Connell was less interested in the family dynamics and more focused on the music personalities that were expected to attend the services. And there were plenty of rockers stepping out of the stretch limos. Without having Russo by the detective's side, however, it was going to be difficult to figure out for O'Connell as to which musicians were unimportant and those that they might want to focus their attention on.

The veteran detective had her badge displayed prominently over her non-uniformed jacket, so there would be no mistake that she was not there for autographs. O'Connell found it amusing that Peterson's former PR firm talked the funeral home into erecting temporary walls to keep the onlookers and paparazzi away. She had total access to the funeral home so none of that was going to affect her observation.

As O'Connell continued to wait for Russo, the detective was fighting the urge to revert back to her teenage days and ask for autographs. With many famous rockers were streaming through the doors, it was hard to keep her own emotions in check. In attendance were Steven Tyler and Joe Perry from Aerosmith, looking as classic rockers should always look. Right behind them were Miami Steve Van Zandt and Max Weinberg from Bruce Springsteen's E Street Band; Bruce himself was expecting to come later. David Johansen from the New York Dolls was writing down something to Blondie's Debbie Harry. Even industry moguls such as Ahmet Ertegun and Clive Davis were next to each other as they walked inside to pay their final respects.

Admiring the parade of rockers walking past her, a rookie cop began calling out for O'Connell.

"Detective, detective. This guy said he knows you? Tony Russo."

As the name 'Tony Russo' reached the nearby rockers' ears at the same time as O'Connell's, some chuckling was heard from the crowd. The detective had forgotten that although Russo's name was as well respected as rock critics went, he was still a critic. There were plenty of talented musicians that had been cut down at one time or another by Russo's merciless music column. O'Connell knew Russo had plenty of other rocker friends in various music circles but it was nothing like the bond that Peterson and Russo had developed.

"I was beginning to think you weren't coming," said O'Connell, as she carefully stepped over the smaller police barricade.

"Between work, family and you, I'm lucky I have any time to get anything done," replied Russo. "I'm doing the best I can. Hey, you know the story behind Leapin' Larry's funeral home, right?"

"Leapin' Larry? Can't say that I do," said O'Connell.

"Old story. Back in the Twenties, Larry Krugman Sr. was a big-time gambler living over in Stewart Manor. And when they arrested him in a raid, overnight he tried to become everyone's friend by turning into some sort of stock guru—you know, the future is in stocks, buy, buy, buy. Then he lost everything in the Crash of '29. People sued him. Others wanted his legs broken.

"That's nice," replied O'Connell.

"I know. But he was one of those Pollyanna types that said you have to keep the faith. But the Great Depression was off and running. Anyway, he saw a way out: down. Jumped right off the top of his house and that's where he got his nickname. He wasn't alone; the town was actually nicknamed Suicide Manor back then. Anyway, his son Larry Jr. vowed never to get in a crazy business like his old man did and opened up this place."

"And you're telling me this because…?" said O'Connell.

"Well, they take great care of the families over the years. Unlike Larry Sr., his son understood the value and importance of friendship and this place has the history to support that. And speaking of history, Caitlin, did you get those rock history books I told you to get?"

"Not yet. Too busy with paper work on this case," said O'Connell. "But go ahead—yell at me for not doing my homework."

Russo smiled. "I'm telling you, if you want to start putting some of the pieces together, it's the best way for you to get started. At least go to the newsstand and start reading MOJO, the UK rock music magazine. Otherwise you'll never understand how it all connects."

O'Connell nodded her head in agreement. "I'll get them tomorrow—promise. But don't get pushy. I'm trying to cover a lot of ground here. And that's why I have you!"

"I know. You keep reminding me," said Russo. "So what's on your mind?"

"Well, if money was not a motive behind Tommy's murder, our man has to be after something else. Now he's got to be associated to the music industry in some way. The killer's access to the studio, the rare guitar used as a weapon. He definitely knows music. But if this guy is as crazy as we might believe, there's a remote chance that the killer might show up here tonight."

"Ok. A musician kills a rock legend then shows up here in person?" said Russo. "I don't see that at all. But you have better instincts for this kind of thing than I would."

"Why thank you," said O'Connell. "What I want you to do for me tonight is observe everyone who's coming in here tonight. Not just the big-time celebs, Tony. I know those names. It's the friends, the writers, the rank-and-file industry folk, groupies. You know, the ones that you've come across over the course of time that I won't recognize."

Russo turned his head away from the detective and glanced at the mourners who continued to head inside the funeral home. In Russo's mind, there was a great deal of skepticism on what O'Connell was proposing. He thought the better plan was to slow down and do the research. The risk in doing something like this was that it seemed to be a fishing expedition, with the NYPD throwing the largest net out there they could find. Worse, Russo was also putting himself out there as their snoop—and an open target—within the rock music community.

"Caitlin, about your plan," said Russo. "Trying to identify everyone at once is one thing. But putting myself out here unprotected like this—is that a smart idea? I'm not a cop, you know. So remind me why I'm doing this again."

O'Connell looked straight into Russo's eyes. "Tony, whether you like it or not, Tommy considered you as a very close friend, so much that he entrusted you to help write his book. But you don't have to do anything if you don't want. I'm learning that Tommy was a celebrity but a private person for four decades that carried a ton of baggage. Without someone like you, well, either the person has to turn himself in or I have to pray for a miracle while I sift through his messy life of his."

"Wait a second!" Russo blurted out. "There have been a million murder cases that have come through your department. I can't believe that this one case rests on me putting myself out on the line."

"It doesn't, Tony," said O'Connell. "I never said it did. But it's people like you that often make or break a case. You're the kind of guy that helps us connect the dots. We're not rock and roll experts, you know."

Before Russo could respond to O'Connell, a hand came up onto his shoulder. It was none other than Ray "DJ Ray" Casazza of WNYR 101.8FM, the legendary rock disc jockey who had been playing rock and roll in the New York metro area since The Beatles landed in New York City back in 1964. There wasn't a person over 40 who had not listened at one time to Casazza's rock radio show. Although he came dressed like a Florida retiree, Casazza was definitely a classy New York music institution.

"How are ya, Tony?" bellowed Casazza in that familiar baritone voice of his. "Sad week for rock and roll. Who's your cute friend?" O'Connell smiled.

"Ray, Detective O'Connell. She's working the Peterson case."

"Nice to meet you," said Casazza as he shook the detective's hand. "You know, this is no different than the John Lennon case for me. I was good friends with John and good friends with Tommy as well. Man, we gotta find the creep who did this. Peterson brought so much joy into this world with his music. We can't just let this guy slip away."

Pointing to Russo, Casazza said, "So you are helping out with the case? 'Cause you know, detective, this guy knew Tommy pretty well."

"I know," smirked O'Connell with her arms folded. She was waiting to see how Russo was going to respond to the disc jockey's comment.

"Well, the detective needs some answers to some questions so I'm doing what I can," replied Russo sheepishly.

"Tony, c'mon. I know you know a lot more than the average person here tonight. Besides, detective, I don't think you want to rely too much on these rockers' memories. Between the partying, the blood transfusions and age alone, I'm surprised how some of them can remember how to put their shoes on in the morning. Tony has a better set of brain cells."

"Good point, Ray," said O'Connell.

Russo said nothing. He wasn't going to discuss his role with the NYPD with a music DJ.

"I'm just glad that everyone is trying to help," said Casazza as he reached into his pocket to give the detective his business card. "If you have any questions, give me a buzz and I'll try to steer you in the right direction. I know just as many rock and roll people as Tony does."

"Well, I'm very happy we got to meet. I will certainly take you up on your offer," said O'Connell.

"Be well, folks," said Casazza as he went over to say hello to one of his favorite friends in the business—bassist Phil Lesh of The Grateful Dead.

It was becoming apparent to Russo that there was no escaping from O'Connell's grip as she pursued Tommy Peterson's killer. He had the music knowledge and connections regarding the former rocker's life that O'Connell so desperately needed.

"Ready?" said Russo. "And let's not have to stand next to each other the entire time, deal?"

"Sure thing, Tony," said O'Connell. "Whatever makes you happy."

# CHAPTER 13

▼

The unlikely duo of Caitlin O'Connell and Tony Russo were side by side inside the funeral home where the late Tommy Peterson was in repose. Because of Peterson's prominence as a top rock and roller, many well-known entertainers were paying their respects to the fallen star. There was, though, a small handful that only valued the evening funeral services as a business opportunity. Although Peterson's mother Eileen had an attendee list of family and friends she sent to Peterson's management company, the firm added too many celebrity types, organizing the wake as if it was a party. As a result, the security became unusually tight throughout the entire evening.

O'Connell unassumingly moved to a corner of the room where she knew she would be able to view the mourners that were attending. With Russo's help, the senior detective began the arduous task of mentally taking names of the countless folks she could identify and then disappear into the bathroom in order to write them down. This technique of hers worked well at mob funeral services where every large-framed, Italian-looking guy looked exactly the same and she couldn't risk taking out a pad and paper there.

Tiring of the frequent runs to the bathroom, O'Connell returned to where Russo was located and positioned herself behind him in such a way that she could jot down her notes without being noticed. The rock critic was amused with her unorthodox method.

"Alright, so how long do you want me to stand here like this for? The entire service?" said Russo.

"No, that's not the plan," said O'Connell. "Hmmm. What I'm thinking is I'll get some more names and if someone really jumps out at you that we should talk to, let me know."

"Too bad you can't videotape in here," said Russo.

"Ah, but we have a camera outside the entrance recording everyone that's coming in," replied O'Connell.

"You do? So why don't we just look at that later and follow up?"

"Well, some folks always manage to sneak in, some don't take all their glasses off, and some people get lost in the crowd. And if the video feed gets messed up, well, then I've got nothing. This is the best kind of backup: direct visual contact with the crowds," said O'Connell.

"Your best bet tonight, Caitlin, is to find one real good person and talk to them. But in the meanwhile, let's see who's here," said Russo. He knew that O'Connell wasn't interested in any of the political folks, movie stars or immediate family members. She wanted names that were affiliated with the music industry, man or woman.

"Ah, here's someone I haven't seen in a while. Bob and Linda Zindle."

"I'm listening," said O'Connell as she scribbled away.

"Back in the early Eighties," said Russo, "those two ran a music management company called BLZ Events. They got involved with some reunion tours from other Sixties bands that they knew personally. They were profitable because the baby boomers wanted to relive their youth again, so they had a good thing going. When interest in getting The Winding Roads back together started in the early Nineties, the band was into it but Peterson. Tommy felt he was done but the rest of the band kept at him, telling him he owed it to them. But Bob and Linda said they were going to do something very different: it would be a weekend Winding Roads convention. There would be rock memorabilia, karaoke contests, tribute bands and capped off the last night by a one-set performance by the band."

O'Connell continued to take notes. She was impressed with Russo's knowledge of the band. How he could remember all of this off the top of his head was amazing. Considering the Zindles were the first two people Russo had spotted, the detective was hoping that she would have enough paper to collect all of this information down.

"Reluctantly," continued Russo, "Tommy said yes—mostly because the rest of the band and management thought it was a brief, painless way to cash in. On the first day of the convention, for some reason Tommy calls up a makeup guy and decides to go down to the convention hall in a disguise. He wants to see what this is all about. He wasn't happy. Tommy spotted a number of guys dressed up like him in numerous outfits he had worn on different tours. And the tribute band's performance was bad enough. But their banter with the audience was almost identical to things Tommy had said in previously recorded performances. That totally spooked him. Tommy had seen enough. He called up John Kenney and said he wasn't showing up at all and left on vacation or something."

"Huh. So the Zindles had no reunion show," replied O'Connell.

"Not quite. Kenney found someone from Tommy's solo band to fill in at the last minute," said Russo. "However, word leaked out on Saturday before Sunday's reunion show about Peterson's no show and fans who had paid a fortune for the three-day event caused a small riot there. Sunday's show went on but it was a poor turnout. The vendors started hassling Linda and Bob, then the convention hall folks was angry at them about some damage that some disgruntled fans had caused. So the Zindles turned around and sued Peterson."

"So what ended up happening?" asked O'Connell.

"Like every lawsuit, it dragged on for a while and eventually both parties settled. The Zindles were afraid that future business in the entertainment world would suffer if this went on too long. Peterson did want to make amends publicly if he was going to do more solo tours down the road. I mean the Zindles had waged a nasty media war while they waited for Peterson to settle."

"Interesting. So why would they come here?"

"Hey, where there's lots of classic rockers, there are lots of business cards to hand out for future tours and conventions. Business first, grieving second. To be honest, Caitlin, I don't even know if anyone even remembers that story other than me," said Russo.

"That's ok. How about some fast quick updates on some of the others standing over there? Or just pick and choose," said O'Connell.

"Let's scan the room fast and I'll start talking," said Russo. As the veteran writer scanned the room, Russo began to fire out names to the detective like a cannon while O'Connell did everything in her power to keep up with him.

"There's John Rosato, guitarist of August March. A classic rock guy from the UK. Big druggie and used to feed Tommy his junk on tour. And over there is Robert Parry, a heavy-duty blues guy. Always looking for a handout, he begged Peterson to let him open up for The Roads. He actually brawled once with Tommy backstage over it. There's the Egan Brothers, Larry and Mike.

Seventies hard rock maniacs who stole some of their act from the Roads and ended up as rivals of The Roads for a time in the Eighties. And that woman back there? Perla, the rock photographer and one-time groupie. Tommy wasn't happy about his appearance in her tell-all book. Next to her is George Rose, the founder of Saffron Records. Gave The Roads their first record deal, which paid the band peanuts over the years. Saffron had to sue The Roads when they tried to leave the label."

"Slow down Tony," replied O'Connell. "Is there anyone here that didn't have an axe to grind with Peterson?"

Russo smirked. "Caitlin, you have to understand that in entertainment, you're only as good as your next release. And if you've been around long enough with a decent amount of success like Tommy had, you end up in situations that you just cannot avoid. He made some good decisions but the bad ones stayed, well, stayed with him for a long time. I guess it's a somewhat forgiving group because nothing ever seemed to stop Tony from doing new projects with some of them. Peterson was a tough cookie, man—he just kept moving forward."

O'Connell was getting a much clearer picture of the types of folks in this room. These were rock and roll *survivors*. Many of them—performers and non-performers alike—that came in and out of Peterson's life eventually worked out any ongoing issues in the constantly changing world of rock music. Regardless, the detective was sticking to her guns that someone Tommy Peterson knew in the music business was not the forgiving type and not interested in working through the difficulties. This person just wanted Tommy dead.

"I hear you, friend," replied O'Connell, "but we want to make the biggest list of names possible—the bigger, the better. So keep going. I'll tell you when my writing hand starts to cramp up."

Russo continued, spewing out names and comments and what they did in the music business. As he continued, the two of them noticed some activity by the funeral home's entrance.

"Huh! You'd think she would have been here earlier," said Russo.

"Who?" said O'Connell.

"Peterson's girlfriend. You know. Indigo."

O'Connell stretched her neck to get a better look at Tommy Peterson's longtime babe. The detective remembered that Indigo had her own reputation in the independent film industry before meeting Peterson. Her reputation in the music business, however, was similar to Linda McCartney: a personality in her own right but always tied into her mega-successful spouse. The hardcore fans and the music folks were not exactly enamored with her. But over time, Indigo's opinionated views faded from view as Peterson and The Winding Roads vanished during the Nineties. O'Connell decided to take Russo's advice and target a discussion with Indigo, the closest person in the world to Tommy Peterson.

"That's who I've got to get to tonight," said O'Connell. "Indigo."

"Good luck," quipped Russo. "I don't think you'll have a prayer here. Didn't she already come down to the station?"

"Yeah, she made a brief statement but I wasn't there. But if Indigo wants answers to who did this to Tommy, she'll talk to me. I'm going over to see her. Wait here and keep taking down more names."

Russo ripped off the top sheet off of O'Connell's pad and kept writing. He was aware that Peterson's mother didn't want Indigo showcasing herself in the middle of a wake but there was no way to keep his live-in girlfriend excluded from the services. So if the detective could slowly work her way into that crowd and get Indigo to talk to her privately somewhere in the funeral home, it would be a successful night.

O'Connell began to move through the crowds as she closed in on Peterson's girlfriend. Indigo was not difficult to find. She was an attractive tall woman with long reddish hair and a white suit, holding court with a couple of rockers, a reporter and some older-looking celebrities. As Indigo turned to talk to another group, O'Connell saw an opportunity and stepped directly into her path.

"Yes?" said a surprised Indigo.

"Detective O'Connell. NYPD. It's very important I talk to you. Do you have a few minutes?" she whispered.

The urgency in the detective's voice took Peterson's girl-friend by surprise. "Right now?"

O'Connell knew the only way she could convince Indigo to talk with her was if there was something that had to be addressed immediately. "Yes. It's critical that we talk now. It will only take a few minutes. Follow me over to the funeral director's office."

"Folks, I will be back shortly," said Indigo to the small crowd as she held onto the detective's hand. O'Connell wasn't sure if it was her approach, the expression on her face or the badge. Maybe it was all three—it didn't matter. In her heart, O'Connell believed the faster she contacted the right people in Peterson's life like Indigo, the quicker she could nab the killer. The detective was genuinely surprised by how responsive Indigo was to her unexpected request.

With the funeral director's permission, the two women entered the dark office and closed the door behind them. It was a large office that looked as if it was frozen in time, with dusty, framed pictures of President Kennedy, The Rat Pack and the 1961 New York Yankees hanging up on the brown paneling that hadn't been dusted in years. But Indigo seemed very comfortable in the room.

"You know I met JFK when I was a pre-teen. My father was very entrenched in the Democratic Party here in New York," said Indigo as she stared at the photos. "It happened so long ago it all seems like it happened in the 1860s rather than the 1960s."

"A lot has happened since JFK was killed," said O'Connell.

"Too much," responded Indigo. "Personally I feel things are moving so fast nowadays that no one has time to sit back and enjoy the moment. All of this technology, cell phones and pagers nonsense. There's no time for people to develop or understand or learn. Everything has to be right here right now. Instant gratification all the time."

"I agree," said O'Connell. "But in certain situations, I think the quicker the information the better. And that applies to your boyfriend's murder, don't you think?"

Indigo looked down at the tiled floor, her hair covering her entire face. "I'm still in a fogbank about Tommy. I'm not sure whether I should lie down in my bed and pull the sheets over my head for a month or go out and yell and scream my head off. I already spoke to all of you police people about what I know about that night. Tommy was a complicated guy with things always evolving and devolving all the time. I'll help you with whatever you need but I think finding this person might be like trying to find a needle in a haystack."

"We're working on a couple of different theories. I know it's hard but try to be optimistic about this," said O'Connell. "What we want to try to do is to zone in on some of the more likely people based on Tommy's past and go from there."

"I have to admit, detective," said Indigo, "I honestly can't think of anyone that would do this to Tommy. You know, he had run-ins with his band, some heated discussions with people in the industry and family squabbles with his ex-wife and the kids. But nothing that wasn't fixable. I read about these horrible shootouts that hip-hop artists have had from time to time. The rock guys never got into that sort of thing."

"Right. And Tommy wasn't really off the radar screen as of late," replied O'Connell.

"Correct. His music was only played on the classic rock stations, the solo tours were very short, the CDs he released did sell but not a lot, and there wasn't a big demand for interviews from the media anymore. Tommy was enjoying the quiet life with me. He was amazed that his friend Elton John could maintain such a high profile year after year. So if anything, I'm more confused about why this happened. He was semi-retired."

"Are you thinking a fan did this and not someone close to Tommy?" said O'Connell.

"Detective, I've seen enough detective shows to know that anything is possible. I have no idea," said Indigo.

"Indigo, perhaps someone Tommy knew wanted to make it look like a crazed fan did it," replied O'Connell.

Indigo stared at O'Connell. "But if that is true, that will still take a long time to figure out, correct? I mean Tommy kept in touch with so many."

"Well, I have a friend of Tommy's working with me on filling the gaps. Tony Russo. And hopefully you could help the two of us after we get all our information together."

"Tony," said Indigo in a disapproving voice. "I know Tommy felt some sort of loyalty to Tony but I've never liked the media. Tony was always mining Tommy for information about any story he was doing on someone else other than Tommy. And Tony paid Tommy back with glowing interviews and favorable reviews on his shows and CDs. I guess I should be grateful that Tony supported Tommy in the difficult times, but I don't think he was being as honest as he should have been. But Tony knew the history of The Winding Roads like no one else so Tommy felt if anyone was going to help him with this autobiography, it was a writer like Tony that wouldn't cause too much interference."

O'Connell was surprised with Indigo's unflattering description of Russo. But the detective knew Indigo was in a difficult spot. She was not married to Peterson and his ex-wife and kids as well as her mother had a legitimate stake to the millions that Peterson had accrued over the years. Indigo's reputation, according to Russo, was she didn't trust anyone and Indigo had carefully invested in things under her own name, in the event that the two of them were no longer together. It didn't matter that they were together for a couple of decades. What mattered now was how Indigo protected herself as well as the legacy of her former lover.

"This is a team effort so we will need your help. There is no escaping that fact," said O'Connell.

"If it's all the same to you, I'd rather deal with you directly. And you know I will be busy this week on this memorial concert I now have to plan with John Kenney in Central Park," said Indigo.

"Understood. I am surprised you're doing this so soon," said O'Connell.

"To be honest, I didn't want to but John Kenney and his label and his mother all wanted to do it. They've already rounded up the band members and some others and they'll be doing an all-acoustic tribute to Tommy. I really had no say in the matter," said Indigo. "That's what happens when you're not the spouse."

"Well, I hope everything works out. And let us know if you hear or receive anything suspicious. We will have a couple of policemen at your place for the next week or so," said O'Connell.

"God, I really don't want to go back there. At least the studio area is on a different floor," said Indigo as she stood up from the chair. "But I guess I have to go back in soon. Our whole life was in there."

O'Connell followed Indigo out of the office and back into the funeral home. "That doesn't sound easy at all. I wish you the best of luck with that, Indigo. We'll be in touch."

The detective headed back over to where Tony Russo was sitting. The funeral home was only going to be open for another ten minutes. As O'Connell approached her new buddy, she was impressed. Russo had written over a hundred names and small comments next to each person on the sheets of paper he had borrowed from her.

"Wow! Now that's impressive. And I think I can actually read your handwriting as well," said O'Connell.

Russo handed her the sheets of paper. "Man, you did forget what time it was. Everyone's gone. But I'm impressed on how much time Indigo gave you. She's not exactly my cup of tea."

"Yeah, I got that impression from her about you as well."

Russo shook his head. "Indigo's a bit of a control freak. She always thought someone was trying to get something from Tommy. You couldn't just be a friend to him without an agenda."

"Hopefully she'll be cooperative," said O'Connell.

"Are you going to try to talk to Tommy's mom too before we leave?" asked Russo.

"No," replied O'Connell. "Not now. From what I've heard about her so far, Tommy's mom was pretty much out of the loop as to what was going on day to day in her son's life. She's pushing 80, you know."

Russo scratched his head for a bit. "I've got to file another story for my publisher. I have to give him something from here to make him happy. So on that note, I'm heading out. So I will see you at the concert, correct?" said Russo as he reached for his coat.

"Yup. We should be there together," said O'Connell. "Let me walk out with you," as she tucked her notes away for safe-keeping. The two of them meandered through the hallway and down the steps of the funeral home, managing to slip through the crowds and gawkers. Some folks were still trying to spot a celebrity leaving the services.

"God, why don't they all just go home?" said O'Connell.

Russo laughed quietly. He knew his former friend Tommy Peterson more than understood what the detective was complaining about. Why anyone had interest in seeing a celebrity walk in and out of a building made no sense to Russo. It wasn't as if one of the rock stars would walk up to a complete stranger, strike up a conversation and then ask them out to dinner. But it didn't seem to matter to the diehard, celebrity-obsessed fans. Getting close to the stars made their day, as they had a bizarre desire to tell their family and friends what celebrities they managed to see, even if it meant waiting for them outside of a funeral home.

*Get a life, folks,* thought Russo. *Get a life.*

# CHAPTER 14

▼

The wanted man wandered out from beyond the police barricades and in a corner of the crowded funeral home parking lot. There were only a handful of cars that were allowed to park inside the space, mostly due to the massive media circus that had descended upon the area. Everyone else had to park at least two blocks away. All of this was for the late Tommy Peterson.

*So this lousy bastard gets Presidential TV coverage for being murdered,* thought the killer. *Guess I'm the one to blame. Too bad Tommy wasn't getting this kind of attention for all the crappy music he was trying to pump out. Man, Tommy should have had it in his will that his estate should spend money on hiring quality security so that people like me wouldn't sneak into his own wake.*

The fugitive dug into his jacket and pulled out a cigarette. Thirty years ago, he never had to carry a pack with him; someone always had an extra cigarette handy. Now he had to travel around with a carton of smokes to continue his nicotine habit because of all the quitters and building restrictions. He stood alone, trying to puff away the tension that refused to leave his body, even as he paid his 'respects' to his victim.

One thing was damn certain. The killer was completely finished with all of the 'phony baloney' handshakes he had to initiate the past couple of hours. The majority of the older rockers that he hadn't seen in many years he enjoyed saying 'hello' to again, like Eric Burdon from The Animals, Leslie West from Mountain, to name a few. Because the murderer's career was incredibly brief decades earlier, it took some of the veteran rock stars a bit longer to remember who he was. He was not uncomfortable with their memory loss until he heard the same musicians say hello to other lesser-known rockers right away. There was nothing he could do to resolve that situation.

Except for the killer, it was widely known that there was a difference between being talented and being successful in music. The smarter musicians back in the early days of rock did one of two things: they either continued in the same music situation for many years while building up their legacy or left the industry and invested in other business ventures with the money they had made during their prime.

Peterson's murderer, however, had done neither. His unfortunate luck and a lack of common sense were mostly to blame. Perhaps circumstances had forced him into a difficult financial situation, as the killer kept trying to salvage a music career in an industry that had pushed him aside. But to the killer, he had a different word for circumstances: Tommy Peterson.

The murderer found the aimlessly wandering police officers amusing. *All these cops standing around doing nothing but crowd control. Not one of them even knows that the most wanted man in New York City is standing among them. What a bunch of morons.* As he finished his cigarette, the wanted man noticed a camera crew that was interviewing a woman detective. She looked familiar but he couldn't place the face. Unraveling a newspaper he had stuck in his back pocket, the killer spotted the name under a picture featured in the latest Tommy Peterson story:

Caitlin O'Connell

*Nice body*, whispered the murderer. *But apparently not that smart. Maybe if she stopped looking straight into the camera and glanced over at me, she would become enlightened and 'see' the answer to her prayers and wouldn't have to do all these 'missing murderer' interviews. But I forgot. She doesn't have a clue as to who it might be. What a pity.*

The murderer also spotted someone else standing only a few feet away from the detective. The gentleman looked even more familiar but he couldn't seem to get a good look at him from where he was standing. The murderer lit up another cigarette and proceeded to get a better angle as to who was with the detective. It definitely wasn't a rock star or the head of a record label. *Who is that guy? I know him from somewhere.*

As the killer carefully inched closer to the subjects, it hit him like a ton of bricks. It was not another detective but none other than Tony Russo, the rock critic.

*Tony Russo. Feeding the NYPD some background on dear old Tommy? That figures. Guess you got tired of bashing artist after artist. Guess there's not much work for an old-time critic hack.*

The murderer always hated rock writers and critics with a passion, especially Russo's unorthodox style of writing like he knew everything about anything. He was once a target once of Russo's nasty reviews on the killer's only solo record but everyone else jumped on his bandwagon. *Rock critics think they have all the answers to what's good and bad*, thought the killer, *even though many of them have never picked up an instrument or tried to write a song.* The murderer wanted music critics to be more like food critics, who could cook and thus appreciated the effort that the chefs spent in the kitchen.

The fugitive turned and walked back in the other direction. He was getting a bit too close to two folks that were trying to arrest him and there was no need to tempt fate. As the killer stuck his cold hands back inside his jacket, he removed the piece of paper that Peterson's girlfriend Indigo had handed him earlier inside the funeral home. It was a special invitation to appear at the Tommy Peterson memorial concert that was being held a couple of days from now in Central Park. Touted as an acoustic show, Indigo wanted him to do some backing vocals with some of the other featured artists.

*She doesn't invite me here tonight but she gives me an invitation. Of course, I don't get to sing a song by myself or play guitar,* grumbled the killer. *I have to be lumped into the rest of the masses and sing something that won't feature my voice. But it's good to see Indigo still thinks so highly of me, that stupid bitch.*

The killer crumbled up the paper in his hand. He was positive that Indigo was part of his undoing many years ago. The fact that Indigo pretended that nothing had ever happened in the past drove him crazy. *How could she have forgotten?* Perhaps she hadn't but to the killer, she was the second half of his 'project.' The murderer knew he wasn't going to kill her near a crowded funeral home. It had taken the murderer a few months just to plan out Peterson's murder. Of course, had Indigo been there with Peterson that night, it would have been a convenient easy two-for-one. Now he had to endure Indigo's endless TV interviews. Hopefully, that would end soon.

The killer pondered another option. *After the concert, will I be able to find an opportunity there to finish off Indigo once and for all?* Nothing was impossible but the security was going to be tight. As part of the talent, the fugitive convinced himself he wasn't a suspect at all. They were focusing on a crazed fan, much like John Lennon's assassin Mark David Chapman. There were even some conspiracy theorists that hated Indigo who suggested to police that she might have had a hand in Peterson's demise, much like those who believed Courtney Love was responsible for Nirvana superstar Kurt Cobain's suicide.

As more and more people began to congregate outside as closing time approached, the wanted man knew he couldn't follow them around to eavesdrop on their conversation. It was time to walk away and head back home. The key issue for the murderer was how to isolate Indigo for just a couple of minutes and finish what he had started with her boyfriend Tommy.

*Think, man, think,* said the killer to himself. *There's got to be a way.*

# T.P. Autobio summary notes excerpts (mid '70s section)

*Our Country*, the documentary that we agreed to back in '75, allowed the public to get an up-close look at what a preposterous bunch of hooligans we had become. We had begun to lose sight of why we started out in the music business and it was all captured on celluloid. I don't know if it was a mistake to do such a film at that point in our career but we did. I guess we were so full of ourselves we didn't care what was going to happen.

When film director Chris Lynch asked us if he could make a documentary about us, we were under the impression that it would be mostly backstage footage, concert clips, an interview or two and some work in the studio. What we failed to realize was that once the cameras started rolling, the footage would be with us forever. And with Lynch being quite diligent in capturing every aspect of our life, we were in for a rude awakening.

*We had just lost Steve Mars forever and we were breaking in bassist Mark Hughes. Because Mark was so different than Steve, the chemistry was not working out so well. Lots of arguing and drinking and carrying on and all of it caught on film. The one-on-one interviews were troubling. Lynch had this habit of harping on the negative and kept trying to draw us out. In the end, some of the comments we made about each other were just downright nasty.*

*To his credit, some of the live performances Lynch captured were among some of the best we had done in years. But when I looked closely at my own performance, I was surprised to see what I looked like. Since you don't walk around with a mirror in front of you, at different stages of your life you think you look a certain way. During this period, I was starting to lose my hair, I had put on fifteen pounds, my clothes looked awful and I rarely made eye contact with anyone. I thought I came off as a tough, skinny kid from New York City. Instead, I looked more like a middle-aged wedding band guitarist that drank way too much at the reception.*

*Although many of our devoted fans seemed to enjoy the flick, the critics tore it apart. Again, part of the problem was that the band itself seemed too caught up in themselves. I believe the "Pin The Tail On The Critic's Ass" game that was filmed after a Los Angeles show guaranteed that the movie was going to be universally panned.*

*I thought the most interesting part of the film, however, was a segment where I came into a music store in Chicago to buy a couple of Gibson guitars. As the store manager sent me to the back of the store to avoid the other 'nosy' customers, there was a 13-year-old kid who was trying out an Ovation acoustic guitar. One of the clerks went to remove him from where he was jamming and I said, "Hey, he was here first. I'll just hang here next to him."*

*If you could see the kid's face, it was priceless. He couldn't speak or play; all he could do was stare at me. As I started to tune up, the kid—his name was Ben, I think—relaxed and asked me a question. He wanted to know what I was doing here in the store. When I replied that I didn't understand his question, the kid said he thought that since I was so rich, other people went out for me to buy my guitars. I laughed, telling him that wasn't true, and ended up doing a little jam together.*

*But that small bit in the movie sort of summed it up for me. I was living in a rock and roll bubble. The kid identified me with private jets, the entourages, the room service, whatever. I had reached a point where I was mostly out of touch with the daily grind. I had no idea of how much a guitar, a car or a pair of boots cost. Someone else either paid it for or I got some freebie from an admiring fan. And when I look back at the songs I wrote during that time period, they were among the weakest I had written to date.*

*Why? Simple—there was no fire in my belly. I had nothing to say.*

# CHAPTER 15

▼

The cops were still trying to estimate the crowd size for the Tommy Peterson memorial concert at Central Park. With the lousy weather and acoustic format, however, they knew it was going to be a subdued show that Tommy Peterson's girlfriend Indigo and Peterson's bandmate John Kenney had co-organized. The two of them had butted heads in the past, not unlike The Beatles' Paul McCartney and John Lennon's widow Yoko Ono. Tonight, however, both Kenney and Indigo understood each other and what Tommy Peterson meant to them and his fans.

The day before the concert was Peterson's funeral, which was open only to the immediate family and Tommy's closest friends. There was a little bit of unexpected hostility when Indigo wanted to speak during the service and Peterson's mother Eileen, who had made all of the funeral arrangements, stood up and said, "There's no talking during this service. Save it for the reporters, honey." With Peterson's children present, Indigo made the wise choice and sat down, remaining quiet for the duration of the services.

Overnight, Detective Caitlin O'Connell typed in all of the names that Tony Russo had given her following Peterson's wake. With close to three hundred names and some brief descriptions as to who they were, most were surprisingly unfamiliar to the detective. But it was something they could both look at together to see if a couple of names stood out among the list. Although O'Connell knew her favorite rock star well, there had to be countless, behind-the-scenes stories that Tommy Peterson was involved with during his 40-year career. She would just have to be patient.

As the detective continued to walk around the perimeter of the staging area, O'Connell wondered if the killer had made an appearance at the funeral home. She had the surveillance tapes of everyone who had attended and the sign-in list, but there were no problems or unusual behavior at the funeral home and the funeral director had not received any threatening phone calls or letters. Still, the detective wasn't giving up on her theory just yet. With thousands expected to attend the memorial concert, O'Connell and the police refocused their efforts to make sure everything was safe for tonight's show.

O'Connell stopped as she rounded the corner of the main stage to dial Tony Russo. The detective knew she was wearing out her welcome with the constant calls to the rock critic. But she was on a mission and knew he wasn't exactly thrilled about his day job at the magazine. Besides, Russo wanted his friend's murderer brought to justice.

"Tony, it's Caitlin. How are you? Where are you?"

"I'm just entering the park now," responded Russo on his cell phone. "I showed them the credentials you gave me so I should be near you in a few minutes."

"Great," said O'Connell. "Hey, I did print out the list of names you gave to me the other night. We're going to have to run through all of them rather quick. To me, it's a bunch of no-names."

"And I also brought the outline and some rough draft passages from Tommy's autobiography. A lot of it won't be useful but I think it will at least help you make sense of some of the other people and stories I know you don't know about."

"Awesome. See you in a few," said O'Connell.

The detective closed up her cell phone. Because of her grueling schedule, O'Connell didn't get a chance to spend much time with a man who wasn't a cop or a relative. Russo wasn't her type, especially since he was married, but it was odd how well they were working together in such a short amount of time. She did overhear Russo's wife complaining to him about the hours he was spending at work and on the murder case. O'Connell didn't want to cause any marital problems but O'Connell had no intention of discouraging his interest. As the detective turned her head to the right, she could see Russo approaching, waving a newspaper in his hand.

"This is so bizarre. We're having a memorial concert for Tommy and the ground above his grave hasn't even hardened yet," said Russo as he walked up next to O'Connell. "So what are they estimating in terms of people for this show?"

"I think around a few thousand but I'm not sure. It's also supposed to rain again and the temperatures are starting to drop," said O'Connell."

"So you want me here today to do the same thing that I did the other night? Take notes, right?" said Russo.

"Yeah, more of the same," said O'Connell. "There's nothing wrong with getting more names. If anything, it will just give us more to work from."

Russo smiled. "By the way, aside from getting heat from my publisher and my family, the word may be getting out among music friends of mine that I'm asking a lot of questions."

"I imagine that's not a widespread fact," said O'Connell.

"Yeah, but it's not helping that it's Indigo who's quietly spreading the word around."

"You know that for a fact?" said O'Connell.

"Caitlin, one of Indigo's assistants put two and two together and after you spoke with Indigo. Her assistant saw us leaving the funeral home together," said Russo.

"Hmmm," said O'Connell. "My chief is not thrilled with this arrangement we have so let's not discuss that with him.

Since we don't know who the murderer is yet, we might have to assume that he might know you're working on this case."

Russo seemed a bit startled at the detective's response. "Great. Now I'm a target?"

O'Connell shook her head. "Relax. I don't think you have anything to worry about."

Russo began to look a little pale. "Caitlin, that's not a very good answer. Maybe I should just stop doing this cop thing and go back to writing."

O'Connell put her hand on Russo's shoulder to calm him down. "Tony, after this concert, we'll have more than what we started out with and you can go back to what you were doing."

Russo knew that the killer was aware that everyone in New York City was searching for him. So unless the murderer had a personal vendetta against Russo, O'Connell was probably right. He would be fine.

"Maybe I just got a little ahead of myself there," said Russo, "but I'm not doing this much longer."

"So let's see if we can find a good position for us where no one will see us together. We can also take a quick peek at the lineup for tonight's show," said O'Connell.

The detective and the rock critic funneled through the usual chaos: the oversized roadies trying to move and position the heavy equipment into position; waif-like models wandering around on their cell phones arguing about why this or that wasn't ready for them today; senior-citizen music industry types (short men donning bad ponytails, tall women using makeup as camouflage) snapping their fingers to the background music over the PA; shaggy-looking photographers, weighted down with three cameras around their necks, trying to find the right spot to set up; and the occasional primadonna rocker, usually carrying nothing more than a water bottle, walking around but saying nothing to anyone. It was a circus atmosphere but without the fun.

Within less than three hours, the makeshift stage was in place. It helped the organizers that a band had played there the night before, so the crew only needed to make minor stage adjustments for the last-minute memorial concert. And as the sun slowly began to disappear behind the tall skyscrapers that surrounded Central Park, Indigo came out to the center stage to address the anxious crowd.

"I loved Tommy Peterson and so did you," said Indigo. "So let tonight's music take you away."

One by one, Tommy Peterson's musician friends came out onstage and performed a song or two written by the late rocker. Some artists brought out entire bands while others came out just by themselves with a guitar in hand. It was a who's who of rock and roll over the past 40 years but it wasn't a joyous occasion. Many of Tommy's fans held white candles that were distributed upon entry into the park with the applause subdued out of respect. A couple of performers struggled with their songs, including one rocker who walked off halfway through because she was unable to keep her emotions in check.

But O'Connell and Russo were not focused on the music. They knew why they had come to tonight's performance and were constantly examining everything that was happening. They had a perfect view that allowed them to observe the crowd, all the performers onstage and the ongoing activity behind the curtain.

Russo, of course, was doing double duty. He promised his boss Johnny Merseburg he would review the concert for *Rock Forever*. But Russo was also taking notes for Detective O'Connell as to which musicians he had identified at Peterson's wake that were here tonight. And who was absent. O'Connell knew she would be little help in that department, deciding to keep a watchful eye on the action transpiring around the front of the stage. The detective was not expecting anything to happen this evening but it was important to be prepared for anything.

As the concert began to wind down towards the end of the second hour, O'Connell nudged Russo with her elbow.

"Tony, let's get down from here and head around backstage. I want to move around a bit and see these folks up close."

With television monitors broadcasting the live show throughout the entire backstage area, Russo knew he wouldn't miss any of the performances for his review if he left his seat. "Sure. Are you zeroing on somebody that you saw?"

O'Connell shook her head. "No. Still don't have anything solid on any one person yet. If this killer is working alone, it's gonna be even harder. But by tomorrow we should have enough for us to sit down and plow through these names and come up with something. Anything!"

"Understood," said Russo. "But why don't we split up? Let me walk around on my own and I'll circle back with you in a bit."

"Deal," said O'Connell. As Russo headed off, the detective began to walk the perimeter of the stage, pretending to be security while carefully eavesdropping on conversations as she walked between the rock stars that were gathering. After bumping into so many of her rock idols the past few days, O'Connell felt a little less awestruck than before. She realized they weren't any different than the famous politicians or pro athletes she had met over the years. And knowing that there might be a killer among them, it was easier for the detective to idolize them a bit less.

Russo, however, was having a slightly different experience. When he walked up to get some quotes from a group of veteran rockers, which included Louis Cosentino from Merging Traffic and Scott Williams of Glenbrook Jam, he cracked up instantly when they all took out their earplugs simultaneously to hear him. However, they didn't find it as amusing as Russo did.

For the veteran journalist, he was bothered by the backstage activity. Aside from the excessive partying, it was clear to Russo that most of the discussions had nothing to do with the life and death of Tommy Peterson. At both the Live Aid and Farm Aid benefit concerts years ago, you knew what people were supposed to be talking about backstage. But the backstage conversations at Peterson's concert seemed more about networking and less about Peterson. Apparently the music folks who were uncomfortable about talking business at the funeral services felt fine about talking business now.

After an hour of wandering around, Russo found O'Connell over by an oversized buffet table in the corner of the main backstage tent.

"How did you do? Come across anything interesting?" said Russo.

"Tony, it's like some big out of control cocktail party for a bunch of old rockers," said O'Connell. "How about you?"

"Much of the same," responded Russo. "I saw some old friends, met a couple of new people. Then again, I wasn't expecting any surprises anyway. By the way, have you seen Indigo at all? She's usually front and center at these things and I haven't seen her lately. Not that I'm looking for her."

"No," said O'Connell. "Not since she left the stage. Maybe she's holed up in a room. It's probably an emotional day for her."

"Maybe, but not to see her at all since she kicked this thing off is unlike her. Tommy's ex-wife and mom are more visible today than Indigo. It's strange not to see her making the rounds."

As the two partners-in-crime were talking about Peterson's girlfriend, they were unaware that Indigo was already in the process of leaving the backstage area wearing a disguise. It was a suggestion made from a friend backstage who told her she could avoid the fans that way when she left the concert.

However, Indigo's friend was apparently no friend at all.

# CHAPTER 16

▼

Indigo bent over to pull up her black cowboy boots—the same ones that U2's charismatic singer Bono had given her as a gift—before she exited the backstage area. Instead of going through the heavily trafficked backstage exit with a police escort, Indigo left alone through a different exit that had been secured by the police. None of the media and fans was allowed within 200 feet of the area, another benefit of the post-9/11 world that the NYPD enjoyed. It was the perfect place for Indigo to leave undetected before the Tommy Peterson memorial concert was over.

Before leaving, Indigo pulled aside a police captain to explain to him why she was wearing a long black wig, dark shades, and a sanitation uniform with a broom in hand. She told the confused captain that everyone in the city was looking to say 'Hello' to her tonight and she wanted to avoid that situation. Sensing some stress in Indigo's voice, the police captain asked if she wanted a police escort home. Indigo declined the offer, stating she and her late boyfriend Tommy walked all over the city without security because that's the way they lived their lives. The police captain shrugged his shoulders and agreed to let her walk out the exit, broom and all, by herself.

As Indigo began to walk undetected through the scattered crowds in the cool evening air, she began to feel the anxiety subsiding that had been with her since the start of tonight's concert. Right after Tommy was killed, Indigo had been caught up in the moment and agreed to doing the show without thinking. What she wasn't prepared for was the aggressive media reporters and the overzealous fans looking for answers. But the press didn't want answers and the fanatics were inconsolable.

Indigo also realized that her stable world was going to change dramatically post-Tommy Peterson—the music party opportunities she loved would dwindle, the free invites to various NYC happenings would begin to evaporate and the money would be there but certainly not like before. With plenty of life and energy inside of her, Indigo would soon have to re-establish an identity of her own beyond her late boyfriend rocker. Dressing up as a sanitation worker was not how Indigo wanted to start out in this new direction, but this was only a temporary adjustment until her new life began tomorrow.

As Indigo made a turn down a darkened path, she heard a familiar voice coming from the distance.

"Hey Indigo, it worked. I'm impressed."

Indigo turned around and there was her "friend"—the one who had come up with the brilliant disguise.

"Well, it won't be if you keep saying my name that loud," quipped Indigo. "How did you ever think of this idea?"

Her "friend" had a big grin on his face. *How stupid is this woman? She plans this show, leaves her own show unescorted knowing full well that her boyfriend's killer is still out there. Tommy always had strange tastes when it came to women but Indigo was definitely at the top of the manure pile. And she still thinks I'm her friend? Had she really forgotten what she had done to me years back?*

"I saw it in a movie once. Plus it works better in the evening anyway. But I'm leaving too. I've had enough for one evening," said the friend.

Indigo smiled. "So you did quite well from what I heard. Sorry I missed it. It's hard jumping up there onstage without much notice, isn't it? Didn't you think Joe Cocker and Don Henley were amazing?"

The killer couldn't believe what he was hearing. *So I did "quite well" but apparently you missed it? Are you complementing and insulting me at the same time? Maybe if I was given more than fifteen seconds to choose a song you might have seen it. It wasn't even a solo. I was singing with eight other people around me. Indigo, you sound just like your dead boyfriend. Clueless beyond description.*

"Uh, yeah," said the friend as he walked beside her. "Just what I expected. By the way, dear, if you really want to steer away from the crowds, I'd head over that direction. I'm heading that way anyway."

"It looks a bit dark over there, don't you think?" asked Indigo.

"Nah, there's more lights right beyond that area," replied the friend. "Follow me."

As they headed out together through Central Park, the friend decided to ask a question that had been on his mind for quite some time.

"You know, Indigo, at the wake, I overheard you telling some people that you have a couple of theories on what happened to Tommy," said the friend.

"I do, but it's really not so much theory as it is access to what I have."

The murderer's heart began to beat faster. *Access to what?* he thought.

"You know," said Indigo. "All that info Tommy was putting together for his autobiography. My theory, if you want to call it that, is that if this person really had it in for Tommy, it had to be something significant. Why else would he have killed Tommy? I have no idea why myself, so what we'll have to do is go back to all the notes, maybe with a couple of people helping me, and see if we can root out who it is. It's not going to happen overnight but it's as good a start as any. I have spoken to the police again but I haven't discussed my idea."

*Is their any truth to what she's saying?* thought the murderer. *I doubt very much they'll find anything in Tommy's book that mentions me but I can't take any chances.*

The two continued their chat as they walked deeper off the walkway and into an area of the park that had more trees and overgrown bushes. Indigo was confused as to where they were headed but she wasn't as familiar with this part of the park like her friend was. The event had obviously distracted Indigo's regular pattern of thinking. Worse, Indigo was unaware of any potential danger.

*I'm running out of time,* said the killer. *Beyond that big rock is more light and probably more people. This belt I have on will work nicely. God, Tommy's murder was so much easier to do—camping out, the tools and weapons at my side, no one to interfere. It was perfect. I'll have to move fast.*

"Wait a second. Where are we now?" said a confused Indigo. The leaves on the ground were ankle high and she could barely make out where she was going. "Do you know where we…"

The murderer lunged at Indigo from behind with his leather belt, knocking her down. Lassoing the dead rocker's girlfriend neck with his belt, he pulled her back towards his chest so she was unable to move forward.

"What the...what...get off....ahhhhhhh," gurgled Indigo. She wasn't the strongest woman in town but the old woman wasn't about to give up without a fight. Indigo could see that the police area she left was only a few hundred yards away. It was now or never if she was going to try and get their attention. Indigo swung her body around and got loose for a second, driving the top of her right foot straight up into her friend's crotch. The killer winced in pain as he temporarily let go of the belt.

"HELP!" screamed Indigo at the top of her lungs.

The murderer knew he had to end this situation right now or he was a dead man for sure. The killer jumped on top of Indigo's chest, driving her back into the ground. Positioning his hands correctly, he jerked her head violently from left to right, breaking her neck. The energy that was in Indigo's body had vanished in an instant.

*You had to make it difficult, didn't you, Indigo? Well, you and Tommy made it difficult for me and you neither cared nor remembered what you did to me back then. But I did. So you got what was coming to do. You miss Tommy? Well now you can spend the rest of eternity next to him.*

But with Indigo's scream clearly heard, a police whistle was blown as the police began running in every direction, including where the murderer was now standing above his second victim. If he didn't get out in the park before they closed it off, he would be caught in a matter of minutes. The race was on.

# CHAPTER 17

▼

"Tony, did you hear that?" said a startled Caitlin O'Connell.

"That scream? Yeah! Clear as day!" replied Tony Russo.

"CODE 217. 2-1-7. ALL UNITS RESPOND IN THE VICINITY BEYOND THE BACKSTAGE AREA," said the cracking voice over O'Connell's two-way radio.

As O'Connell and Russo ran towards one of the police captains in charge, they heard him telling a group of police officers something that they couldn't even imagine.

"Peterson's girlfriend Indigo just left about five minutes ago wearing a sanitation uniform as a disguise off in that direction," said the captain. "Hard to say if she's actually the one in distress but we're fanning out to see who's in trouble."

O'Connell bolted out of the back security area with Russo running close behind. "Of all the stupid…"

"Caitlin, where are you going? And why am I running?" said Russo.

"Tony! Indigo in a disguise? It's got to be her that's in trouble. I know it," said O'Connell as she continued to run. "Someone stalked Peterson when he was murdered and the same person was here tonight and went after Indigo. We've got to find this guy tonight!"

Russo was not in the same physical shape as O'Connell, but more importantly, he was not a cop. He wasn't trained to chase down criminals and make an arrest. He was a writer and was nervous about where he was headed.

"So what am I supposed to do if I bump into this killer?" said Russo as he tried to keep up with the much faster detective. "You have a gun, he probably has a gun, and I have nothing."

The detective stopped abruptly. "If I was in a bikini on a beach and I saw something happening to someone in the ocean, I would jump in. It's what people do, Tony, when other people are in trouble. It's what I do. So keep running or stay here. I don't care."

O'Connell darted off, with Russo deciding to run as best as he could. Standing alone in Central Park right now was probably not a good idea for the unarmed rock and roll writer.

\*　　\*　　\*　　\*

The murderer was moving as fast as his old legs could carry him. This was exactly what he didn't want to happen when he decided to murder Indigo this evening. In his warped mind, it was all perfectly laid out. *I accept the invitation, keep my eye on Indigo the entire time, talk to her and find out what she was up to, make the suggestion of a disguise to sneak out of here, leave before she does to make it seem like a surprise that we bumped into each other, direct her to an isolated area, and finish her off. She seemed like a weak little thing—how did I know she'd put up such a fight?*

The nighttime atmosphere aided the killer, as he easily disappeared into every nook and cranny that Central Park had to offer. But he still had to locate the concrete wall that surrounded the entire park, hurdle the wall without being detected, and then disappear onto the busy streets of New York City. The problem was the murderer wasn't entirely sure how close he was to the park's wall.

As the killer came out to a small clearing, he now remembered where he was. The park's scalable wall was only a short distance away. But should he run and possibly draw attention to himself or should he casually but briskly walk through the park, hoping to get to the wall before the cops stopped him?

The wanted man chose the latter and began to walk down the path even as the distant police noises were getting closer by the second. The murderer knew what was at stake and could not risk being detected by anyone. *I have to be cool. Just pretend that you're back onstage doing your rock and roll thing and you haven't a care in the world. They have no idea who they're looking for so just keep on moving forward.*

As the killer walked past a number of people along the concrete path, no one recognized him. They were focused on all the police activity that had descended on the murder scene off in the distance. He kept moving, knowing that the longer he stayed in Central Park, the greater the chance that someone might be able to identify him. Although it was dark, he left his hat and shades on. The eyes were always a dead giveaway to a person's identity.

Two policemen on horseback galloped by the murderer as the radio blurted out something the killer was shocked to hear: "MURDER SUSPECT IS NOT IN CUSTODY. MAY BE A BACKSTAGE GUEST. BE ON THE LOOKOUT FOR ANY KNOWN CELEBRITY OR SOMEONE DRESSED FOR A STAGE PERFORMANCE."

He wasn't dressed like Prince or Elton John—just a blue shirt and jeans—but the murderer took off the hat and jacket as a precaution. More important, with the killer hearing the words 'murder suspect' he knew the cops had now arrived at the crime scene. *They found Indigo's body. But why would they say that it might be a performer? I have to get out of here and fast. As soon as those cops disappear, I'm running straight for the wall.*

*       *       *       *

O'Connell was talking to the captain on her two-way radio as she ran with Russo through the dimly lit park.

"Captain, like I told you a couple of minutes ago, I don't have a clue who it is but someone in the music industry—possibly a performer—who had backstage access tonight might be the killer."

"I heard you the first time, detective. I got the word out already. Be smart out there," said the captain.

Russo was slowing up. The rock journalist hadn't run this much since he had to run the mile under eight minutes at school. "Caitlin, I'm dying out here. My lungs are ready to explode. What are we doing now?"

O'Connell stopped for a moment. "Tony, if he gets out of the park, that's it. We've lost our opportunity. So let's keep pushing. Head up over this way."

Taking a deep breath, Russo continued to follow the adrenalin-fueled detective. When he started out in the magazine business, some of his buddies from high school became cops and firemen. Almost all of them were retired now after putting in their 20 years and had taken up new careers in real estate, Wall Street, security, coaching—you name it. And here was Russo, running with a cop in NYC after a killer instead of writing a story about a rock concert. This recent lifestyle change didn't seem right.

O'Connell looked down from a giant boulder with Russo. The cops with their flashlights were beginning to stop anyone along the park's paths.

"They're wasting time," said O'Connell "They should be…"

Off in the distance, O'Connell saw something flash near the park's concrete wall. It wasn't from a flashlight but more like something that was reflecting off a person's body. As O'Connell took out her night binoculars, she zoomed in to take a closer look. It was a large man flinging his legs over the wall.

"HEAD FOR THAT WALL!" screamed O'Connell as she jumped off the boulder. "Officers, up there! Someone's headed over the wall!"

Russo and O'Connell sprinted down and over towards the spot where she had seen the reflection. Russo could hear the cops calling in for backup, as several police officers were sprinting behind the two of them. O'Connell wasn't positive that it was the killer who had scaled the wall but this was as close to a possibility as anything else. As the other officers caught up to them, Russo could see they all had their gun holsters open.

"You guys aren't going to start shooting, are you?" said Russo to one of the cops.

"Who the hell are you?" said one of the officers.

"He's with me," barked O'Connell as they came up to the wall at the same time. "Guys, I think he jumped right here. Let's go!"

In unison, they all jumped the Central Park concrete wall and onto the sidewalk that ran along Fifth Avenue. As they fanned out down the street, the area was practically empty—just a couple walking off in the distance with their dog and an old man out for a stroll. Even the car traffic was relatively light. And without a close ID of his face or what the suspect was wearing, it was hard to know who they were looking for and which direction he had gone.

"Spread out and see if anyone is hiding in the bushes or stairwells down those two side streets," said O'Connell. The frustrated detective had hoped that they could question this mystery man. Was he Indigo's killer—or even Peterson's killer? It didn't matter now. *He was gone.* As O'Connell continued to look around the street, she realized Russo had not cleared the wall with them.

"Tony?" barked O'Connell. "Where are you?"

"I'm back over here," said Russo. "Look what I found."

As O'Connell walked back over to the park's wall, she could see Russo's arm slowly stretching into the air. The rock journalist had a laminated backstage pass to the concert in his hand. The detective concluded the light from the street lamp had reflected off the badge, which was what the detective had spotted from the boulder, and accidentally fallen off from the possible suspect as he jumped the wall. Russo's rising arm motion reminded O'Connell of the Lady of the Lake sword tale from the King Arthur book when the mysterious hand emerged with a sword Arthur needed to become king. O'Connell now had her own version of *Excalibur*.

# CHAPTER 18

▼

The killer desperately gasped for air as he hid inside a train tunnel. He had no idea whether the police would walk the three long city blocks and down south on Lexington Avenue where the Number 6 east side subway train stop was located. But the wanted man had no choice but to wait it out underground for a while. Two other people, waiting patiently for the next subway train to arrive, were way down at the other end of the subway platform. As far as he could tell, they did not notice that the suspect had just stepped off the platform and into the dark and dangerous subway tunnel.

Running any distance was painful. He was an old rock and roller, not an athlete. His sides were in terrible pain and his chest felt as if it was about to collapse from his body at any moment. But in a few minutes, his body would relax and he wouldn't have to care. The killer had succeeded once again at killing his intended victim and the temporary pain he was now experiencing would be history.

As the prime suspect leaned up against the cold, subway wall, he was angry. He had spotted that woman detective jumping the walls and heard her call out Russo's name before he darted down the street. *So that O'Connell woman was after me again,* thought the fugitive. *And that jerk Russo was with her as well— had he retired from writing and joined the NYPD? It doesn't make any sense. I know he was tight with Peterson but so what? Are they hoping that by recruiting a rock critic they will be able to find me?*

Off in the distance, a train was pulling into the station. The killer stepped back into an alcove a few feet away from the tracks and closed his eyes as the train roared through the dirty tunnel, sending debris in every direction. Although he was frightened by the train's proximity to himself and the loud, metallic screeching from the metal wheels, the murderer was more scared when he had been spotted jumping over the concrete wall in Central Park. It was too close for comfort. But the deed was done and it was time to figure out a way back home.

*Alright. Gotta think here. They don't have a suspect and couldn't have spotted my face, although I know who they are. That woman cop O'Connell has no idea who I am. But Russo knows me from music. Don't think they're smart enough to put two and two together but they must know this isn't random. Probably someone with access to Tommy. I'm betting that by now, they think this is some guy out for revenge. Aren't we all?*

As the murderer looked down at his shirt, he noticed the blue lanyard around his neck was still there but his backstage access tag was missing. His name wasn't on the actual tag itself and didn't believe his fingerprints were on it when they placed it around his neck. It probably disappeared somewhere in Central Park while he was sprinting, but the odds of anyone locating the tag were slim. To the fugitive, it was now another piece of city garbage lost somewhere amongst the leaves.

The killer's mind kept racing. *What if these two jerkoffs end up calling me down to the station? I snuck into the funeral home but I was at the show so they know I was there. I may be a drunk but I'm not an idiot. I have some time before they go through any list. Maybe I should pack up and get out of New York. Gotta think.*

Off in the distance, the fugitive could see a subway dweller approaching him very slowly. The disheveled man looked to be in his fifties and was walking with a cup in one hand and a blanket in another. There were many homeless people that were afraid of the city's shelters and chose the city's underground transit system as a place to live on their own without interference. With nowhere to run, the murderer stood quietly, hoping that the drifter would continue on past. Instead, he stopped.

"You're new. Are you looking for a spot? Plenty down there and to the left," said the man.

"No," said the killer to himself, "I'm just standing here taking a rest."

"The name's Colin. Got a funny voice," said the vagrant. "Not from around here, right?"

The murderer did not like the line of questioning. "I don't feel like talking much now, if you don't mind."

"Fine. See if I ca...hey, wait a second." The man squinted and looked closely at the prime suspect. "You look familiar."

The killer's heart began to beat rapidly. *A man who had shunned society and chose to live in a subway tunnel remembered my face? This homeless man actually knows me? There's no way this slob can possibly remember who I am. Impossible!*

"Something with music, right? I had my own band before the drugs set it. Right? You're in music. I never forget a face."

Ever so slightly, the murderer turned his head to the right and stared away from the homeless person. *I've got to get out of here but I can't leave right now. What am I going to do about this guy?* In a corner of the wall lay a two-foot-long piece of metal left by a track worker. The killer realized he would have to do again what he had just done an hour ago earlier to Peterson's girlfriend.

"I had your record. Something with stones on the cover," said the man.

That was all that the killer needed to hear. The unsuspecting vagrant was putting together pieces of the mysterious killer musician that the NYC cops who were pursuing him were unable to do. The murderer reached over to the long metal shaft as the beggar was desperately trying to jog his clouded memory and remember whom this stranger was.

The vagrant suddenly opened his arms wide. "I got it!" he said. "You're not from around here! You're that…"

The murderer whipped his arm high into the air and then down onto the homeless person's head with the metal shaft, rendering him unconscious upon impact. Quickly looking in both directions, the killer dragged the derelict's body into the middle of the subway tracks. *No one's here,* he thought. *The next train will be here in a few minutes and I will be gone by the time they find him all over the tunnel.*

The fugitive took the weapon and slid it down a small crevice. He then took his blue lanyard that had once held his backstage pass and dropped it down the narrow hole as well. As he approached the platform stairs, he looked up first to see if anyone else was nearby. With no one in sight, the killer quietly stepped back up onto the train platform. There was a different couple now standing way down on the other end but they could not see him. The killer's timing was perfect, as he heard yet another train approaching the station.

As the murderer walked past the unmanned token booth and up the exit stairway, he could hear the train engineer honking his horn furiously as he pulled into the station. It was apparent to the train driver that someone was laying on the tracks and was not going to move out of the way of the oncoming train. The killer then heard someone scream from the station's platform. As expected, some of the derelict's body was easily visible to the unsuspecting couple that had been waiting at the far end of the platform.

But only the murderer knew who that unfortunate person was. It was someone with a very bad sense of timing.

# CHAPTER 19

▼

John Consoli, the chief of detectives at Caitlin O'Connell's precinct, stared at the laminated tag laying on his desk. After a week of dead ends, the police were finally in possession of something that might lead them to both Tommy Peterson's and Indigo's killer.

"So there's no name attached to it or any clear fingerprints but I think your hunch is right, detective. It's likely someone affiliated with the music business," said Consoli.

Russo could see O'Connell beaming with excitement. His friend's hunch was not a crazy one after all.

"Sir, I do have an unofficial list of those who were backstage," replied O'Connell. After the possible suspect escaped, the detective bolted away from Fifth Avenue and over to the concert organizers for a list of those who were on the backstage access list.

"That's good, Caitlin, but my guess is if this maniac is the same guy who murdered these people, he may have been smart enough not to put his name on any list or use a different name," said the chief.

"True. But we haven't gone through all the video cameras either," remarked O'Connell.

Consoli smiled as he placed the single piece of evidence from Central Park back down onto his oak desk. Although the gray-haired police veteran was a very persuasive person with his six-foot-four, 250-pound frame, he was not getting through to either person in his room.

"It's Tony, right?" asked Chief Consoli.

"Yes."

"Tony, I've known O'Connell's family for years. We worked in the days where there wasn't a ton of oversight and we supported each other and got to know the families and the history going way, way back. Now Caitlin's whole family I've known for ages. And they all have had one common trait among them—they always look at every possibility at a crime scene until they drop from exhaustion. Most of the time it has worked. But when it didn't, they drove us all crazy in the process. And she's no different."

"Excuse me, sir," interrupted O'Connell. "I…"

"Hold on," blurted Consoli. "So now this celebrity couple is dead, but we don't know for sure if he's ready to crawl back into the hole from where he came. But there's no time to analyze hours of footage that may lead nowhere or track down every single music celebrity type going back 40 years who have been flying out the past couple of days in every direction. Let's nail down quickly who had an axe to grind with these two victims and root this guy out before dragging the whole record industry down for questioning."

Russo raised his hand. "Well, we have been doing some research."

"Really?" quipped Consoli. "Where's all the history notes on these two victims? Russo, I know you don't work here but if you know these music folks well, get the right people in front of Detective O'Connell and let's see some results. Contact Peterson's current and past management, get some files and correspondence, get some leads. He's taken time to plan his attacks, but I'm beginning to think this guy thinks he's invincible by now."

"I think with Tony's help, we can dig out a suspect," said O'Connell.

"Well, the worst kept secret around town is there's some sort of music connection to the murders," said the chief detective. "But let the newspapers say what they want to say. It doesn't take much in this day and age for conspiracy nuts and the press to take hold of a double celebrity murder case and cause trouble. So we need answers fast."

"I agree," said Russo. "Remember Brian Jones of The Rolling Stones and Nirvana's Kurt Cobain—some think those two were murdered. We don't need those stories again."

O'Connell smiled. "See what I've created? A junior detective."

Consoli stared directly at Russo, even though he was not amused by O'Connell's comments. "I don't know what you're talking about, Tony. I'm not a rock and roll expert. We need your help but the last thing I want is a civilian playing 'Rookie Detective.' Be smart and help OUR detective in getting the answers she needs to close this case. And I better not see any of these office chats inside your magazine while you're with us. You got that?"

Russo stared away from the chief of detectives. Eventually, Russo knew he would pay tribute to his former rock star buddy by writing a great book about his rock and roll reporter experiences someday. But for now, the old-time rock journalist knew he had to be smart about what he was going to write for his magazine.

"Understood," said Russo.

"Again, what we think so far is we've got a tall, white guy somewhere in New York City possibly connected to the music industry that had some sort of falling out with both murder victims," said Consoli. "He may or may not be from New York City but we're thinking yes because he knew how to disappear without a trace. We should check all those in attendance who are from the city area and try to get a list of suspects ASAP. I don't care who you call or where you have to go to get it. Just get in done!"

Chief Consoli opened the door and left his own office to run over to another meeting regarding the high-profile murder cases. As O'Connell and Russo walked out far behind the chief and down to the street, both of them knew it was time to consolidate their information.

"It's 3pm already. Where do you want to head now?" asked Russo.

"I have another motivating place for us to get our minds together. CBGBs."

Russo put his hand over his face. "You and the rock-themed locations. I cannot you picked that place. You know I got punched in the stomach there years ago."

O'Connell folded her arms. "You'll have an armed escort, which you won't even need at the club in the middle of the afternoon. But Tony, it's my favorite club in New York City. The smell, the stories, the look. Maybe you've forgotten?"

Russo looked back at O'Connell with a blank stare. "No, I haven't forgotten, Caitlin," he said. "I just thought a nice quiet library might be more appealing about now."

As the two sped off to the famous 315 Bowery rock and roll address, Russo dialed his wife on his cell phone. He would be late for dinner once again.

# CHAPTER 20

▼

The unmarked police car that Caitlin O'Connell was attempting to park in Manhattan's lower east side neighborhood fit in well. With the rear passenger window slightly cracked, two of the four tires missing their hubcaps and paint peeling on top of the hood, her "temporary partner" Tony Russo was convinced that no one in their right mind would break into her vehicle.

It had been more than twenty years since Russo had stepped foot inside the legendary CBGBs, the last of the edgy Seventies rock clubs. The last time he had visited the club was back in the early Eighties for a record release party for a UK band slated to be the 'next big thing' in town: The Card Cheats. Taking their name from a song off The Clash's timeless record *London Calling*, they were readying themselves for their first-ever US tour. Many who had once called CBGBs 'home' in NYC were in attendance, such as David Byrne from The Talking Heads and Patti Smith, to name a few.

Russo remembered his buddy Tommy Peterson giving advice that night to Gary Sherman, the band's charismatic guitarist and songwriter. Apparently, Tommy's cautionary words failed to work for the newcomer. Only a couple of weeks into their tour, Sherman accidentally overdosed on heroin at the age of 24 and that was the end of The Card Cheats.

"I know this trip seems a bit out there," said O'Connell as she placed her hair up in a bun before entering the club, "but I don't feel like sitting in a stuffy library when we have so much rock and roll to talk about."

"Man, I guess you really need the right atmosphere to work," said Russo. "But I hope we're not going to be here all night."

O'Connell laughed. "I love this place but even I have my limitations, Tony."

As they entered CBGBs, they found a small table inside the rock club. It was only 4pm and all that was going on at the club was a couple of young bands that were unloading and testing their band equipment for their show later on that evening.

"Tony, did I ever tell you the first time I played here?" said O'Connell.

Russo had a feeling that he was in for another long music story from the detective. "No you didn't but go ahead. Get it off your chest."

O'Connell ignored Russo's sarcasm and continued. "Well, after begging and pleading for a slot, my band got the first one, 7pm, with a bunch of other bands on a Thursday night. Anyway, when we arrived, they told us they needed to move us to the 11pm slot because some record guy wasn't waiting that late to see the 11pm band play. So we get onstage and the place, which was somewhat empty at 7pm, was packed at 11. Being friends with a lot of cops growing up, they all came down to support us and began to chat "CAIT-LIN!" over and over before we even played the first note. I got so excited that when I ran up for the first number, I tripped over the stage monitor and fell straight into the crowd."

Russo began to chuckle. "And you hadn't done anything yet."

"Nothing," said O'Connell. "One of my cop friends, Frank Brady from Jamaica, says, 'Heyyyyyyyy...whaddya doing down here? You're supposed to be up there. Now get your butt up there and play me something.' And he proceeds to throw me back onstage, guitar and all, and I crash into the bass drum. Everyone is laughing while my band is in shock. So I get up and say into the microphone, 'Thank you...and good night!' and that was it."

Russo smiled politely as he drank from his beer. "Ah, the ultimate rock and roll sucker punch. A band has one great club gig date and they try to keep that spirit in every place they go next. But it never lasts."

"Anyway let's get back to thinking about what we came here for," said O'Connell.

Russo reached down to get his notes out from his bag. "Hey, you were the one who started this conversation. Not me."

"You're right. I just got distracted with my story. Sometimes I wonder how I get through the day." O'Connell unfolded her own binder of papers and tossed on the beer-stained table. "Now we've been taking a ton of notes on everyone. We have a list from the funeral home, another list from the concert and your Peterson autobio outline. So why don't we dig in and talk about some of the key issues or problems Peterson may have had, look back at the lists we have, and make up a smaller list of people based on the stories? Then we can try to narrow down who we need to follow up with."

"Okay. I have here a few key one-liners that I jotted down that should save us some time," said Russo as he pulled out a different sheet of paper from his jacket. O'Connell took the crumpled paper and began copying down what he had written:

> *Ed Sullivan Show mgmt fight—mid 60s;*
> *Everything Is Nothing tour problem—late 60's;*
> *Paternity case—mid 70s;*
> *BLZ management probs—early 80s;*
> *Testifying against mob guy—early 90s*

"Cool. Let's start with the first one you have," said O'Connell. "The band's managers got into a fight with Ed Sullivan. Why would that be relevant? That was 40 years ago."

"Hey, you asked to dig some stories out," said Russo. "So I'm trying to find a few that might have some historical relevance. The Winding Roads got a slot on what was the hottest show to be on back in the Sixties—*The Ed Sullivan Show*. After The Beatles made their appearance and swept through the States, every band wanted a shot at doing that show. Remember, there were only a few TV stations back then and there was no satellite, Internet or cable.

"So Ryan Guttridge and Joe Acevedo were their managers and they were not a trustworthy team. They had this 'I'm your buddy, I'm your pal' thing but in the end they were only out for each other. Just real creepy, sex-starved guys pretending to be honorable men. Anyway, late in '67 or early '68 the band was set to do a song called 'Bad Politician' and someone from CBS tells them that they have to change a line in their song."

"You're kidding," replied O'Connell.

"Not at all. The Rolling Stones with 'Let's Spend The Night Together' and The Doors' 'Light My Fire' ran into this issue on this show with their songs. Now Ryan and Joe, instead of talking with the band about it, lose their minds one hour before the band is supposed to go on the show and start screaming at everyone and end up in a fistfight with the stage crew. One stagehand got cracked in the head with a chair, they call the cops, and the two of them are arrested and taken off the set. Tommy is livid and didn't even care about the line they had to change. But Sullivan comes up to them and says something like, 'Sorry, boys, maybe next week' and walks right past them. As it turned out, The Winding Roads were later told they were banned from doing the show."

"All because of the two managers?" said O'Connell.

"Yup. So after their managers make bail, the band fires both of them. The show was the last thing they had scheduled before going on a European tour, so it made sense to do it then. The two sued the band but when Acevedo broke from Guttridge and settled his case with the band, Guttridge felt betrayed and ended up with nothing. Later on Ryan got caught up in all sorts of vices, especially alcohol. Joe died a few years back but I know Guttridge is around in the area as he does an interview from time to time so he's probably easy enough to locate. I know he's had some contact with Tommy as he's mentioned in Tommy's notes in passing but I'm not sure what that was about."

"Guttridge, by the way, was not on either of the attendance lists. Now you have down 'Everything Is Nothing tour disaster' listed next," said O'Connell.

Russo took another drink from his warm beer. "There were a lot of things that upset Peterson over the course of time. But any problem that directly affected his music really set him off. So *Everything Is Nothing* comes out and it's a big hit for the band. Both the two singles and the record are charting very well in the US and the UK and the band is feeling confident. However, there was debate on whether the band should go out on the road by themselves or team up with another band. Tommy was getting nuts about the stage show since it was a big cost to include some interactive elements of the stage show. I wasn't around then but that's what Tommy told me. The rest of the band just wanted to play the songs without all the distractions but Tommy felt the fans were expecting something bigger and better than before."

O'Connell could see Russo was on a roll. The information she desired was literally pouring out of him.

"So the US tour starts up but they are struggling with getting their groove together. They decide quickly to postpone the rest of the US dates and zip over to the UK to get into shape at some small venues. But on the second UK date, one of the women who performed onstage with them is raped after one of the post-show parties somewhere inside the arena. Back then, a lot of those stories got crushed because the theory was any woman backstage had to be a groupie just looking for action. The difference this time was the woman that was assaulted had joined them in the UK and was the daughter of a big business tycoon."

"I remember reading something about that once," said O'Connell. "Who was it?"

"Marcus James and his daughter Sunshine. Anyway, James threatened to shut down the whole UK tour through a media campaign he launched against The Winding Roads. Pretty brutal. James told the press that the band was responsible and that his emotionally scarred daughter was not given adequate security and protection. Some of the venues in the UK began to cancel their dates under pressure. Bob Wittman, their manager, decided to cancel the rest of the UK dates and then rebooked a bunch of shows back in the US. But throughout the Seventies, anytime The Winding Roads would try to launch a UK tour, James would step up his attacks."

"I'm assuming Marcus is dead but Sunshine is still out there," said O'Connell.

"Don't know her status at all," said Russo. "But yes, he's long gone."

"Again, I don't have either person on my lists," said O'Connell as she dug into her bag for another pen. "But she's going on it. Next is…"

"A paternity case. Well, Tommy was a rock and roller and, like many of them in his generation, he had his share of fun with the ladies. Except this story is not one of them," said Russo. "For some reason, Tommy had this thing for women in wheelchairs. He told me once that he always felt bad that his aunt, who was a beautiful woman bound to a wheelchair due to a car accident, always had a difficult time dating anyone. Anyway, Tommy met this handicapped woman Marisa in Paris after a show and ended up having a romantic weekend."

"A handicap fetish?" replied O'Connell. "Maybe I don't want to hear anymore about this."

"Yup. And she got pregnant. Had a baby boy. But Marisa developed serious complications due to her situation and she assumed Tommy would pay for all her costs. But Tommy denied even knowing this woman, which sent her into a rage. Remember—he's with Indigo at this time."

"That sounds like trouble," said the detective.

"Yeah, Tommy was using this head instead of the other head," replied Russo as he pointed down to his crotch. "Some organization heard about Marisa's situation, they got her healthy again, and she sues him. Since Peterson vowed never to step foot in France again, it seemed nothing would come of it. Then in the mid-Nineties at some art gallery down in the Soho area, Tommy is confronted by this big, lanky kid, saying, 'You know who I am? I'm Marisa's boy.' And kept saying it over and over until he was escorted out of the gallery. The kid began to harass Peterson by showing up at private functions and Tommy ended up having to get an order of protection against his own kid. Finally the kid went back to France. I thought I remember hearing that Tommy made peace with him or something like that but I'm not sure."

"Now that's a good one," said O'Connell. "We'll have to dig out his name. Maybe he's back in the US."

"Yeah, I guess anything's a possibility," said Russo. "But I don't have his name."

"We'll find it. Now I heard the story about the BLZ people—The Zindles. They were there at the wake, as we know, but they seem a bit remote. But what was this mob story about? That sounds intriguing."

Russo sat back in his chair. "I'm glad you're finding a lot of this very amusing but it's a sad story."

"Yeah, but it's clear that Peterson, as much as he liked to think of himself in very flattering terms, was a bit of a knucklehead at times, Tony. You can't deny that. I mean I know he got caught up at an early age in the rock and roll thing but he didn't have to go on living that lifestyle of his forever, right?"

"True," said Russo, "but he was genuinely a good guy that had faults like everyone else. But because Tony was a rock star, when he was at the top of his game, even the slightest thing had much bigger consequences for him compared to you or me. You're an open target as a rock star. It's no different than what all the big hip-hop stars are going through today."

"Understood," said O'Connell. "But let's debate this later. I wanna hear about this mob story right now."

"Just so you know," said Russo, "this was a story that was not very public and Tommy tried to keep it that way. Tommy said he wanted to write about it in his autobiography but was afraid of something bad happening to him if he did. Instead, he wrote the incident down separately from the book and was going to decide later if he was going to include it in the book or not. Let me dig into this folder."

Russo pulled out scraps of discolored paper, flattened white napkins and a stack of cardboard drink coasters. O'Connell knew journalists as a whole were a bit eccentric when it came to taking notes. But the items Russo was pulling out was more than a bit strange. As Russo looked up, he could see O'Connell staring at him.

"By the way," Russo said, "the discolored paper and napkins are Tommy's notes, not mine. Only the binder paper is."

"Much better," laughed O'Connell. "I was starting to get nervous."

"Let's see here," said Russo. "During the last tour that The Winding Roads played together—not the reunion tours—one of the touring trucks was stolen in Boston. Peterson happened to be outside smoking when two guys jumped in and drove off. Tommy got on the phone immediately and several miles away, they caught one of the drivers. Peterson's management then got a call from the band's attorney and said that one guy's last name is DeZatini, a violent New England mob family. A newspaper guy got wind of the story through a roadie friend and wrote a small story about it.

"The mob does not like press coverage," said the detective.

"No they do not. The next thing Peterson knew, he got a message at home saying that he would have 'a difficult time playing guitar if his hands were missing.' But Tommy said that as long as the police assured him that these guys were going away for a long time, he would ID the other if they caught him. They did and Tommy picked the other one out in a lineup. Now Tommy lucked out 'cause the two were suspects in multiple murders as well so they're doing life. Soon after, almost all of the DeZatini family was arrested for something big and they shut down. But the old man of the mob family said on his deathbed that he hoped one day someone would take care of that 'rocker' that put his two boys away. I remember Tommy's attorney telling Tommy that the rest fled to Sicily. So I think a mob hit was unlikely but possible. I don't think you'd find their names on your list either."

"Nope," said O'Connell. "Not on the list. But there was a threat. Remember, we have to check out everything."

It was now 7pm and the first local band, Ginger Moon, wasted no time in kicking into their first song at full volume. Twenty years ago, neither one of them would have cared much about how loud any band was. But O'Connell and Russo were working on a murder case together and couldn't hear each other. They grabbed all of their papers and moved themselves to the back of the club. Five minutes later and more yelling to each other, the meeting in CBGBs wasn't working. It was time to pack up.

"Follow me," said O'Connell, as she headed out the club door and right next door to CB's Gallery where an acoustic duo, The Message Cookies, was playing. They sat down for a final beer together.

"Tony," said O'Connell, "I guess I was a bit optimistic on finding a name. Forget the Zindles story and the mob story for now. I'll contact their old manager Ryan Guttridge and see what his story is. After that I'll try to look into that woman Marisa and her son's name. Don't you have a writer friend that can help you out with some rock history details about that '69 tour they did?"

"Yeah. I'll call this rock critic that's a old friend—and past rival—of mine," said Russo. "Don Bart. He's the best when it comes to rock music history. I can go through some of these other names too and see if I can make some sense of this."

O'Connell chugged the rest of her beer as she stood up to leave. "I remember you telling me earlier that you'd be crashing at your mom's place in the West Village. Keep your cell phone on just in case something comes up. Deal?"

Russo nodded his head in agreement, finishing off his beer as the two walked out of the club together. They both had their research to do tonight, so for Russo, it was easier for him to crash in Manhattan at his mother's apartment.

"Wish me luck," said Russo as he flagged down a taxi.

"Remember, keep your mouth shut about the details," yelled O'Connell as she walked towards her car. "You're a smart reporter, right? You know what I'm talking about!"

Russo saluted her as he slid into the cab's black vinyl back-seat. He was amazed by how complicated Tommy Peterson's life sounded after telling just a few of Tommy's stories to a stranger. The general public bought his albums, caught a show or two when Peterson was in town, and read a couple of tabloid headlines, but they knew nothing about the day-to-day life of a career rock and roller. That was a world that only a selected few ever got to see.

The cab headed over to Morton Street on Russo's directions; his Mom's place was over there and only a short walk from Peterson's old brownstone. After Russo's father had passed away several years ago, his mother chose to leave the quiet suburbs and head back into Manhattan. The city's many distractions allowed her to move on with the rest of her life and revisit the neighborhood that Russo's mother had originally come from.

Maybe the white picket fence was missing, but there was nothing Russo enjoyed more than having a home-cooked meal at his mother's place.

# CHAPTER 21

▼

Tony Russo had never been to Don Bart's apartment in Battery Park City but there was a first time for everything. He had called his old rock journalist friend the day before and Bart was more than happy to help. This morning, Bart called Russo back to say he now had to get over to his place by 10am at the latest because of a prior commitment he had forgotten about. Without eating or showering, Russo headed quickly over to Bart's place.

Both Russo and Bart had traveled in the same rock circles for almost two decades. But Bart, who was twenty years older than Russo, always made a point during any debate amongst other reporters that HE was there when Chuck Berry and Elvis Presley were starting out and HE had the best perspective of rock music than anyone else.

However, when new bands like Led Zeppelin and The Clash preferred Russo's company to that of the old man, the accessibility that was denied to Bart soon led to reassignments and less topical stories and eventually his dismissal from *Rocker Roller,* the magazine that he had toiled at since its launch. But Bart turned his unemployment time into creating a music best-seller—*Rock and Roll From The Inside Out*—and made a fortune. After the success of his rock history book, Bart landed a teaching position at Manhattan College, which was where he was now employed. And loving life.

After finding Battery West Gardens, Russo parked his car in a space down a side street and headed inside to take the elevator up to the 24th floor. Upon reaching 24M at the end of the hall, he rang the doorbell. The black metal door opened up and there stood Bart, wearing a Rolling Stones *Tattoo You* concert tour T-shirt.

"Nicely faded shirt," said Russo. "Why, may I ask, are you holding on to that rag?"

Bart smirked. "Well, it's sort of a reminder of the last great record tour The Stones did."

Russo's eyes widened. "I don't know about that, Don. The Stones have had some of the most profitable tours in the past dozen years or so."

"You're not listening…again," said Bart. "I didn't say 'successful' tour. Let me ask you this—minus their greatest hits releases, what new original recordings from The Rolling Stones have *you* bought since *Tattoo You?*"

Russo couldn't lie to Bart. He knew that Russo had not purchased an original record from the rock legends since *Tattoo*

*You* came out back in 1981. It wasn't that those subsequent Stones records were bad but they both preferred the Jagger/Richards cutting-edge compositions that were written back in the Sixties and Seventies.

"Ah. So you got me again. Feel better?" said Russo.

"Much better," said Bart. "I do this to my students in class whenever I get the chance. I put this shirt on knowing that you would say something about it the second you walked in."

Russo shook his head in disgust. He was totally set up and didn't see it coming. As he glanced around Bart's place, his one-time rival's apartment was sort of what he expected—the décor was definitely mid-Eighties and the walls were covered with rock photos featuring him in his glory days. Russo then followed the slender, gray-haired man over to the balcony. His apartment overlooked the rebuilding of The World Trade Center site.

"You know I was here on 9/11 and saw the whole thing happen," said Bart as they both gazed out onto the hallowed ground just a few blocks away.

"Man, that must have been awful to watch," said Russo.

"You know the worst of it, Tony, was that I'm watching people running in and out of the Towers. In and out. It was chaos. And then all of a sudden, Tower One was just…gone. 110 stories. Poof! Then this giant dust cloud heads right towards my building. I slammed the storm door shut but the dust was coming in through every vent and crack. I holed myself up in my bathroom with some food and my useless cell phone. I didn't know what had happened to the other Tower until a few hours later."

Unaware of his friend's 9/11 experience, Russo could see Bart was not the same crazy man he had been a decade or so ago. Apparently 9/11 up close and personal was much bigger than anything he had experienced in the music world.

"But you did fine, right?" said Russo.

"Yeah, but I eventually left and stayed over at my son's place in Jersey for a couple of weeks," said Bart. "He came back in with me three weeks later to clean the soot and mess. But I'm staying. I'm a New Yorker, I love the music here and I'm not going anywhere else. But enough about me. What's on your mind, Tony? What's this rock music project you're working on?"

Russo was stunned by how fast Bart's demeanor could change by saying the words "rock music." Bart was one of the last in a dying breed of rock history journalists. And although many of the rock musicians Bart had followed from the beginning had either stopped performing or had died, he knew how it was all connected. The key in talking to Bart, however, was that he needed to avoid telling him about the police investigation he was assisting with. Saying he was working on Peterson's book would give Russo the right lead-in to what he was looking for.

"Well, I'm trying to salvage what's left of Peterson's autobiography. In light of all that's happened, Tommy's mother wants me to spearhead this project and also write something biographical at the beginning about what happened this past week," said Russo.

"Yeah, that Peterson and Indigo double murder brings back memories of Sid Vicious and Nancy Spungen. What a mess that was, remember that?" Bart was referring to the former Sex Pistols bassist suspected of killing his girlfriend in 1978 and then died a few months later from a heroin overdose in New York City. "You know I heard that not only do they think someone from the music industry might be responsible for Tommy's death but the NYPD's got some music person working on the inside trying to find this lunatic."

With his best poker face on, Russo wasted no time in responding. "Yeah, I heard that too. Who knows, right? I mean the New York papers and the tabloids are coming up with something new every day."

"True," said Bart. "I know you lost a good friend in Tommy. But about his book. If I help you out in any way with this, make sure you mention me somewhere. Are you going to get paid to write this book?"

Russo was a bit put off by Bart's insensitivity but he himself was serving up yet another lie, as the Peterson book was not even close to being finished or published. "Yeah, although I think most of the proceeds will be going to Tommy's kids. I'll have to write my own book one day."

"Better start soon. It takes a lot longer than you think," said Bart. "So let's get back to what you want to ask me. We're talking about Tommy Peterson and The Winding Roads so I scanned my files on them. Did you have something specific you wanted to ask me?"

Russo opened up his pad. "What do you remember about the *Everything Is Nothing* tour that The Roads did back in '69 and '70?" said Russo. "I didn't know them personally before the *My Country* tour in '74."

"1975, Tony. Anyway, it was certainly an exciting time for rock," said Bart as he stared up at the ceiling fan. "The album came out between the alpha and the omega of rock shows—the successful Woodstock festival in New York in August '69 and that disastrous Altamont show in California in December '69. I remember The Roads were in a bad way in '69 money-wise. They were at a point where expenses were exceeding revenues big time and their new record was gonna be a 'make or break' release. Influential, possibly, but if it was critically acclaimed and a commercial flop, that might have been it for them. But that didn't happen and they smoked through the Seventies."

"But the UK tour was a disaster after Marcus James' daughter got raped after a show. The press had a field day with that, right?" said Russo.

"Good notes there, Tony," said Bart. "Yup, I got several calls from their label begging me to write some positive pieces on the band and all that. I told them it wasn't up to me what to write.

You know, we get our assignments and we went off to get our story. Not their story! But Tommy was upset, as I recall. He called me about the whole incident. But I don't think he was devastated."

"No?" said Russo. "Why not?"

"Hey, you knew Tommy. He was the consummate rock and roller. He gave long interviews, he was a maniac onstage, an extremely creative songwriter and a real character when he wanted to be. So when anything came along that he didn't understand, he'd get a little nuts and paranoid."

"I'm not getting what that has to do with the tour," replied Russo.

"Well they wouldn't have even gotten to the UK if the first leg of the US tour hadn't got so screwed up," said Bart.

"Meaning…?"

"The band's manager, Bob Wittman, had no idea what he was doing. Although Peterson had gotten crazy in the past dealing with his ex-managers Ryan Guttridge and Joe Acevedo, Wittman was trying to figure out how to best support the record and keep Tommy happy. But Peterson was now getting all sorts of advice from every possible angle. Like Indigo."

Bart had this information right off the top of his head; he wasn't even looking at his notes anymore. He was a living, breathing rock encyclopedia. Why hadn't he come to visit Bart right from the beginning?

"Anyway, Wittman wanted another act to go out on the road with them from the beginning. The Winding Roads was a bit shaky after not playing much together and an opening band could bring in more bucks and stabilize things on the tour. When Peterson got wind of who Wittman wanted on the tour, he reluctantly agreed. Then the opening band had personnel problems. Along with Indigo's advice, Peterson closed the door on the band. Indigo told Tommy he thought the opening act was bad news. The two bands were friends but potential rivals, according to them. So I don't know why Wittman even suggested them in the first place."

Russo was confused. "You haven't mentioned who that band was."

Bart was laughing. "You know, for a guy who's writing his autobiography, you have to know that band's leader. I mean Tommy booted him and his band into rock oblivion after they got kicked off."

Russo rubbed his eyes and began to think. A rival of Tommy's that had his career killed off by Tommy Peterson. A music industry person. Someone who had known Peterson well. But this story was nowhere in Russo's papers or Tommy's notes. If Bart was working with O'Connell and had told her what he was hearing right now, this person would be at the top of the suspects list.

"Who are we talking about? What's his NAME?" exclaimed Russo.

"Calm down, Tony. You know who this is, right?" Bart reached into his folder and pulled out a picture.

Russo knew exactly who the man was and began to text message his intern over at his office. He had hit the jackpot.

# CHAPTER 22

▼

It had been years since Detective Caitlin O'Connell had been out to Montauk. The address given to her on Ryan Guttridge through the police database was sending her to the furthest point on Long Island's southern fork. From Manhattan, it was an easy three-hour drive.

O'Connell had not spoken to her buddy Tony Russo in several hours but figured they would be able to cover more territory by splitting up the work for a day. Getting additional background on the scenarios Russo had laid out the other day was critical in the case. Of course, the detective wasn't thrilled about visiting a potentially ornery drunk but she was the cop. Russo was better off working in a safer environment.

As the detective drove out on the congested Long Island Expressway, she began to daydream back to a summer weekend when her college buddies decided to drive out for a benefit concert that singer Paul Simon was co-hosting somewhere in the Montauk area. Just before her rowdy friends were about to approach the fishing village's traffic circle, she spotted the most famous of the overnight stays: The Memory Motel.

To the average person visiting the quiet beach resort, the motel looked like any other motel. But O'Connell remembered her classic rock tracks and jumped out of the car and ran over to the bar to see The Rolling Stones shrine she had heard so much about. The original bad boys had spent time a great deal of time in the mid-Seventies with other celebrities, especially part-time resident/artist Andy Warhol. Up on the wall was a montage of the band, recording track sheets and other rock tidbits from their 1976 *Black And Blue* record. O'Connell stared at the wall for a few minutes. If only she had the chance to meet the Stones there one night. Would she have been memorable enough to be one of the ladies mentioned in their 'Memory Motel' song?

The detective slapped herself gently on her cheek and focused on the road and why she was going there in the first place. Ryan Guttridge was The Roads' manager during much of the Sixties but fell out of favor along with his partner Joe Acevedo. But Acevedo was dead now so he was useless to her. Although Guttridge sued the band after he was fired, Guttridge may have been in contact with Peterson. And if Guttridge wasn't out there in Montauk, would they have to put an all points bulletin out on Guttridge as a possible suspect?

Turning left onto Montauk Highway in East Hampton, O'Connell blazed through the overpriced, snobby stores, slowed up to take a peek to see who was playing at The Stephen Talkhouse in Amagansett and rolled the windows down as she began the desolate drive out to Montauk. When the main road forked, she instinctively headed to the right onto Old Montauk Highway, otherwise known as the "bumpy road" to her. Her father used to love scaring everyone in the car during their frequent visits by driving on the monstrous hills on the swerving road. O'Connell realized after she took the first giant hill that it wasn't as much fun when you were by yourself.

The address took the detective somewhere north of the traffic circle but situated back by one of the many lakes sprinkled throughout the fisherman's village. Using her trusty Suffolk County road map from college, O'Connell had no trouble finding the small brown and white cottage. She parked on the street and surveyed the property as she began walking up the dirt driveway. As O'Connell turned towards the front door, a voice yelled out from the backyard.

"Who's at my door? Timmy?" said a quivering voice.

As O'Connell peered around the corner of the house, she spotted an old man lying out uncomfortably in a hammock with a 20-ounce can of beer sticking out from between his legs. From the picture Russo had shown her, the detective was pretty sure she had a match.

"Mr. Guttridge?" said the detective.

"Yes?"

"I'm Detective O'Connell from the NYPD. I'm here investigating the murder of Tommy Peterson and his girlfriend

Indigo. I understand you were The Winding Roads' former manager. Can I ask you a few questions?"

Guttridge leaned back in his hammock. "You have got to be kidding me. So let me get this straight. I was The Roads' manager more than three decades ago and you want to ask ME questions? You folks must be desperate. Does it look like I'm a suspect?"

Although Guttridge's slovenly appearance and sloppy living conditions did seem to back up his statement, the detective was trained never to take anything for granted during a homicide investigation. Anything was possible and a good detective explored every possible option.

"I didn't say you were a suspect. But you are aware of the murder case, yes?" asked O'Connell.

"Yeah, yeah, it's all over the TV and the papers," said Guttridge. "How could you avoid it unless you were in a freaking coma? I'm basically housebound now so all I've got is the boob tube and the papers to keep my brain from going soft."

"Housebound?" inquired O'Connell.

"Yeah. I've got problems with my hips," said Guttridge. "Apparently all my drinking has caused all sorts of problems or something like that. But I don't have the money or insurance so I'm pretty much screwed. I knock down some painkillers my buddies get for me. I don't even own a car anymore 'cause it's too hard to get in and out of. So why are you here again?"

It was obvious that Detective O'Connell had hit a roadblock. Ryan Guttridge was the furthest thing from a suspect. This man was clearly incapacitated most of the time. But she had already made the long trip out to his house, so O'Connell figured it was worth asking a few questions to fill in some of the other gaps she had about Tommy Peterson.

"Well, we have been doing a lot of inquiries and background on Tommy Peterson and we'd be very grateful if you could help us in any way. His killer has not been apprehended yet and you'd be doing a great service to the community if…"

"Oh please," said Guttridge as he attempted to sit up in the hammock. "Spare me the dramatics, dear. If I had my health and was still living in Manhattan somewhere, you would have already picked me up for questioning."

O'Connell bit her lip and continued. "Mr. Guttridge, we need a great deal more information and I'd appreciate it if you could cooperate. I know you wouldn't feel comfortable down at our police station. So I'd much rather do this in your house."

Guttridge fell straight back into the hammock again. The frail-looking man barely had the strength to carry on an argument with a persistent detective, let alone taking a trip into New York City. "Fine. Help me up and let's go inside to talk," said Guttridge as he reached out for the detective's hand.

O'Connell extended her arm and pulled the former Winding Roads manager out of the hammock with ease. Hobbling up his walkway, Guttridge led the detective through his rickety front porch and into his small living room. Upon entry, O'Connell had thought she had stepped into yet another wing of the Rock and Roll Hall of Fame. Every square inch of the four walls was covered in Sixties memorabilia: gigantic posters of past gigs by The Winding Roads; photos of the biggest rockers, models and actors from the Sixties with Guttridge in each one of them; a broken Fender Stratocaster signed by Jimi Hendrix; a faded white denim jacket signed by everyone in The Moody Blues, to name a few.

"Ryan, this stuff on your wall is pretty impressive. Do you have any idea what some of these things might be worth?" said O'Connell. "You could get those new hips you wanted if you sold that Jimi Hendrix guitar."

"It's worth nothing to anyone but me," said Guttridge with a nasty tone. "I was in London and backstage at a show of his after Jimi had one of his great shows. Anyway, one of his roadies brings in this broken guitar after the show ended. It was not repairable. Jimi had told them to toss it because he had others to play. I immediately took it out of the garbage but Jimi sees me out of the corner of his eye. Jimi asked me what I was doing picking through his garbage. I said jokingly, 'I lost my ticket stub and I needed a souvenir.' Hendrix gave me that great smile of his and wished me luck with the band. It was a shame what happened to that kid. There was nobody like him, before or after."

O'Connell loved those classic rock stories from the past, but she had come out to Montauk for one reason and one reason alone—to find answers to the unsolved Tommy Peterson case. Guttridge's rock and roll stories were definitely entertaining but would have to wait. The detective decided to take a risk and share with the former manager her thoughts regarding the unsolved murders.

"Mr. Guttridge, I'd like to share with you what I'm thinking. I have reason to believe that both murders may have come from someone within the music industry. And since there was no money or property taken in either attack, I strongly believe that these murders were pre-meditated and the act may have been one of revenge."

"Revenge, huh? I'm not sure about Indigo, but the line forms to the left and down the block if you're looking for possible suspects regarding Tommy's murder," said Guttridge. "Peterson was a rock superstar for a long, long time. When the band broke up and the music industry kept changing on him, he still had all of that baggage trailing him since the early Sixties minus some of the big money he used to make. I mean he was still living quite well but compared to what some of these rap guys get now, it was chicken feed. He had a lot of debts and people to pay off."

"Did you have any contact with him recently?" said O'Connell.

"I never really broke contact with him," said Guttridge.

"But you sued him."

Guttridge laughed out loud. "Caitlin, everybody sues. It's part of being famous and wealthy and all of that other good stuff. I felt I was entitled to X and the band and their attorneys thought Y. I got a little bit something but it wasn't much. Tommy and I had some nastiness for a few years, but Indigo and I kept in touch. Eventually the three of us went out to dinner as early as a couple of years ago."

"So you were on good terms with both of them?" said the detective.

"Yeah. Why the surprise? Is someone telling you something different?" said Guttridge.

"I was given a story about some fight the band had at The Ed Sullivan Show back..."

"Lord, won't they let that stupid story rest?" exclaimed Guttridge. "I even saw that mentioned on some video show called '100 Most Outrageous Rock Fights' and I never laughed so hard. Joe Acevedo, my partner, and I were trying to stick up for the band and it backfired. But you would have thought we killed someone. It was that prick John Kenney, their singer, who got the band to dump us. By the time we left the band, The Winding Roads were already beginning their slide downwards."

"According to my notes, I think they had a pretty successful run after you left,' said O'Connell.

"*Everything Is Nothing* was already being worked on when we left," said Guttridge. "That record definitely got them out of their obligations to their creditors but that was their last big critical success. They made their cash off the touring and merchandise because the Seventies and early Eighties records they were releasing weren't remotely close to the great stuff they had put out when I was running things."

The detective scratched her head with her pen. "Have you thought much about the case at all?" said the detective. "You did say you have been keeping up with some of the story."

Guttridge leaned back and finished off his second beer. "Yeah, but like I said, Tommy had a ton of friends and enemies. Like many stars in his situation back then, Tommy made some good and bad choices. All the major bands did. I do know he had some kid with another woman that wasn't his wife that was seeking him out. Tommy also mentioned he had some problem up in Connecticut with some mob family, but he didn't elaborate on it much."

O'Connell already knew both of those Peterson stories but was surprised at how much Guttridge still remembered. The former manager and former rock icon had a falling out after the Ed Sullivan incident but the two of them had remained friends even after they had parted ways. The rock music industry was a gigantic one, thought O'Connell, but it was very difficult to let go of the past. For both Guttridge and Peterson, there was no need to stay angry forever.

"Can you think of anyone we should follow up with? Is there anyone you think that might have been looking to settle a score?" asked O'Connell.

"Dear, there are so many people to remember…and forget. That would take me a lot of time to think about. There were so many who were in the mix of things when The Winding Roads took off. I mean the bands like The Roads that made it did so with some talent, good timing and a little bit of luck. I don't think I will ever understand why some folks made it and others did not," said Guttridge.

"That's sort of what I'm getting at, Mr. Guttridge. Maybe there was someone who had a chance to 'make it' and had a business disagreement or a personal matter with Peterson," said O'Connell.

"That had to be some disagreement then," said Guttridge. "Sorry I can't be of more help. You're covering a lot of years here and I don't have the greatest memory. But if something comes to me, I'll buzz you," said Guttridge.

"I would appreciate it," said O'Connell, as she gave him her business card.

"Hold on a second, dear" said Guttridge. "For all your hard work, let me give you something from my collection." He walked over to the corner of the room and pulled out an old record from an oversized crate. The plastic-covered album was Pink Floyd's 1973 breakthrough album *Dark Side of the Moon*, complete with band stickers and wall posters that were originally packaged when it was released.

"This record stayed on the Billboard charts for 14 years. Not months. Years," said Guttridge. "This was back when record companies actually gave a crap about the artists they were representing. When you bought their latest release, you felt like you were buying a small piece of them. You probably don't have a turntable but it's one of the best ever. And all four members—Waters, Gilmour, Mason and Wright—signed this baby."

"Ryan, it's very impressive but I really can't accept things like this on a case," said O'Connell.

"How about after the case?" said Guttridge.

"Maybe after…sure," said O'Connell, knowing she would not be back at his house again.

The detective shook Guttridge's hand, handed the Pink Floyd record back to him and headed down the driveway to her car. She was certainly expecting a much worse situation when she visited the band's former manager. Unfortunately, the frustrated detective was not any closer to finding out who had killed Tommy Peterson and Indigo. Maybe something would come to Ryan Guttridge later on and he'd give her a name that she could use. Any name would do.

Any name at all.

# CHAPTER 23

▼

"Johnny! Guess who heard from Tony Russo?" yelled Susan Barkin, the executive secretary to Johnny Merseburg. A loud noise came from the publisher's office, which Barkin knew was the familiar sound of a big chair smashing up against a metal radiator.

"Susan, get in here!" bellowed Merseberg. The rock music publisher could see everyone in town was writing about the Tommy Peterson and Indigo murders: the newspapers, Internet blogs, weekly tabloids and media magazines. And the one magazine that had the upper hand on this story—his *Rock Forever* publication—was fed up with their "scoop" reporter. Russo had been ghost writing Peterson's autobiography before he even started at the magazine so Merseburg assumed he had a lock on a great story from Russo.

But after Peterson's murder, Russo was essentially useless. As a monthly, Merseburg's magazine was already at a competitive disadvantage but Russo's lack of communication was only making things worse. So far, all Merseburg had was one small news story from Russo and that was it. The other writers had to make up the difference after Russo snuck out of the office again to play Cops and Robbers with the NYPD.

Barkin, a one-time pro football cheerleader who went the corporate route by becoming the longtime associate of Merseburg's, ran in as fast as her old legs could carry her. Although she liked to view herself as a competent assistant, Barkin was as thick as a piece of wood. Worse, the hours of makeup foundation just to make herself presentable to her boss proved she had little self-esteem. But knowing Merseburg had finally received some news on Russo was all that mattered in her world.

"What are you standing there for?" yelled Merseburg. "Where is Tony?"

"Tony emailed his new intern Ed Mooney and was asking for information on this person," said Barkin. She handed the piece of paper over to him. Merseburg grabbed it out of her hands and stared at it for a couple of seconds. He then opened up his Internet browser on his computer to search the name.

"I know who he is," said Merseburg. "Well enough to have said 'Hello' to him at Peterson's concert the other night. I even got his recent info. I want to see what a search on Yahoo brings."

"Johnny, if you're doing a search," said Barkin, "you might want to use…"

"Shut up. Did I ask for your opinion? You know I'm a loyal brand user, a Yahoo shareholder and I know a top executive there. Plus the website has never failed me. What else did this kid Ed tell you about Tony?"

"That was it. Ed told him that he'd do a search on this guy's name and Peterson's name together for Tony and Tony would call back later on his cell to find out what information Ed had," said Barkin.

"Did he say where he was?" said Merseburg.

"No," said Barkin.

"Ok. Tell Mooney to come into my office right now. And get me some fresh coffee, will ya? GO!"

While he waited for the intern to arrive, Merseburg added Peterson's name into the search, hit ENTER and looked carefully at all of the top results. Based on what he knew of this musician, the middle-aged eccentric publisher was not expecting much at all. He had thought about the thousands of rock artists from the Sixties who thought they were somebody but ended up as very small footnotes on the Internet.

There were only a few references that popped up, such as a mid-Sixties festival and an indie solo CD of his for sale on eBay. Then there was something that was a bit different than the other two—an article regarding concept albums that mentioned the musician as one of several lesser-known people who had been working on this type of musical format. More important, in the main section of the article alongside the great Sixties rockers, Tommy Peterson's name was listed.

Merseburg stared at the screen for a moment. Was there a 'creative' connection to Peterson and this other rocker? *But why was Tony Russo asking for information on this guy?* Yahoo's search engine had the ability to pull a ton of information from a million sources. But because of this artist's obvious inactivity—or a lack of interest—there wasn't anything else to be found.

Ed Mooney knocked on his door that was already open. "You wanted to see me, sir?"

"God, stop calling me sir," said Merseburg. "We're not at some tightly wrapped investment banking firm. Ed, you want a promotion here, two things have to happen right now. One, only you, Susan and me know about the name Tony just called in about and it will stay that way. Two, you need to go into every major music magazine from around 1964 to the early Eighties and find out everything you can on this guy. The fact that Tony's not communicating to us is pissing me off. My gut feeling is he's trying to do a story with someone else and he's using our resources to get it done and get paid."

"Ok," said Mooney. "I'll get started right now."

"Good. And call me every single time you find something," said Merseburg.

Mooney walked out quickly as Barkin reentered the office. "Johnny, you really think that is what Tony is up to? I mean he's a seasoned reporter."

"Of course not, Susan. Thank God I don't pay you to think. I sent the kid on a wild goose chase. I mean if he finds something, great. But the kid doesn't know his ass from his elbow, so by promising him a promotion, he'll keep his trap shut."

"Ok. So now I'm lost," said Barkin. What are you thinking about this guy that Tony's looking for?"

"Good bye, Susan," said Merseburg.

Barkin shrugged her shoulders and closed the door behind her as she left the room. The publisher smiled as he stood up from behind his desk. Picking up his Rickenbacker 12-string guitar Roger McGuinn made famous with The Byrds, Merseburg strummed an E minor chord over and over as he looked out his office window.

Merseburg had lied to both the wide-eyed intern and his useless secretary. He knew *exactly* what was going on with Tony. Merseburg knew very well that Russo wasn't doing a feature piece on Peterson for another magazine. Nor was Russo doing a follow-up article for his magazine. Merseburg knew the cops had a music insider working with them because Russo had already told him that a detective had been pestering him for information.

From where the publisher was sitting, Russo had now given Merseburg, via the unsuspecting intern, the name of what was probably the prime suspect in the Peterson murder case. *Why else would Russo call in for this washed-up musician?*

With a quick spin of his mighty Rolodex, Merseburg looked to see where he had put the musician's info. The "mystery man" was a New York resident and not a surprise to the smiling publisher. Without wasting a second, Merseburg grabbed his jacket and car keys, slipped a small handgun into his waist and ran out the door. He would write the story on the suspect himself, turning it into a news piece by breaking the biggest story in town.

If that meant keeping the wacko musician at bay with his gun until the police arrived, that was fine by him. Merseburg's reputation for being the story rather than covering the story had preceded him. However, he knew this story would undoubtedly top them all.

# CHAPTER 24

▼

*Man, this feels good.*

The hot shower had done wonders for the killer's aching back. After a twenty-minute shower, the wanted man stepped out of his basement shower stall and over to his adjoining basement recording studio. Sitting in his oversized music studio control room chair with his original music—the only music that would ever run on his machines—blasting at full volume, the murderer could not believe all that had transpired in a week's time.

*Let me see if I can remember everything in the correct order,* thought the killer. *After several months of planning, my decades-old dream finally came true by offing the one and only Tommy Peterson. At Peterson's wake, which I had attended just to make sure the loser was dead, the lovely Indigo asks me to participate at his pathetic memorial concert for Tommy, at which I am only allowed to sing back up since I am part of the 'forgotten musicians' group. Since I also blame the selectively forgetful Indigo for making Tommy's decision for him years ago, I pretend to be*

*Indigo's friend and suggest she get into a clever disguise so she can leave the concert without being noticed. I catch up with her in the middle of Central Park and end her sorry existence as well. After evading New York's finest—ha!—by hiding out in a subway tunnel, I end up taking out a vagrant who was probably one of a handful of non-musicians in the world who still remembered me.*

The fugitive looked at his watch. It was almost noon and it was time to turn on the midday news. He spun around and turned on the television that was suspended from the ceiling in the far corner of the studio. To his surprise, NBC's local TV news veterans Chuck Scarborough and Sue Simmons were doing a special one-hour broadcast related to the recent murders. It was widely known that New York City was very proud of its murder rate being at a 40-year low. But city officials were more than concerned about another "Son of Sam" type murderer roaming around the Big Apple.

"Good afternoon," said Scarborough. "There has been a recent development in the Tommy Peterson murder case. Although a police manhunt has failed to uncover any suspects regarding the murder last week of rock icon Tommy Peterson or his girlfriend Indigo, who was murdered just before Peterson's Central Park memorial concert had ended yesterday, a homeless person was killed by an oncoming 6 train at the 68th street station. However, police have confirmed that the homeless man was beaten over the head with a blunt object first and mud footprints left on the subway platform match the ones left at both Indigo's murder scene and at Peterson's apartment."

*My boots*, said the murderer, *my boots*.

An older-looking police captain was now being interviewed on the TV about the ongoing investigation:

"These boots are apparently a rare set of English-made boots with a very specific pattern. We have called in several shoemakers to help us identify the type of boot and have already contacted all of the shoemakers in the tri-state area to see if anyone has brought this specific boot in for repair."

The murderer shut the TV off and the fear switched back to laughter. *Oh, this is priceless. I haven't brought those boots in for repair work in years. Good luck, detectives. Maybe I'll get lucky and they'll arrest some poor soul in the middle of the night with the same pair of boots and they'll torture the poor bastard for hours.*

As he turned away from the television, the fugitive felt safe and comfortable within the confines of his Garden City house. The well-known Long Island town was an affluent one, boasting three golf courses, plenty of shopping, and outstanding public, parochial and private schools inside its borders. Known as a great place to raise families, the killer did not feel out of place on his busy street, as there were many other retirees throughout the village.

The wanted man lived by himself for several years in his older brother's house after his brother moved away to Florida, taking full possession of the estate after he died. Not wanting to be bothered, the fugitive decided to tell one neighbor shortly after moving in that he was a retired salesman from the UK and he was also battling cancer. He knew the nosy neighbors would be smart enough to leave him alone after that. If they wanted to have a block party during the summer, he'd gladly sign the list for approval but would not attend. He would keep to himself for the duration.

The killer was slightly upset about the TV broadcast. There was nothing he could do about the media but he wasn't a serial killer out to take on the world and all of its evils. The murderer had simply waited for his time to strike back at the two people he despised so many years ago. Tommy and Indigo had to go and that was that. The subway dweller, however, was an unforeseen situation but it had to be dealt with. And now it was time to go back into seclusion.

The one benefit he had from being in a mortgage-free house by himself was the finished basement that the murderer had converted into a home studio by taking out a home equity loan. Reaching down to a box, he took out a reel that was marked PHAEDRUS and walked over to the Studer A80 tape machine to ready the reel for playback. After the label dropped the killer's band years ago from their roster, he managed to steal all of his master recordings from his band, which included his unfinished *masterpiece* as well as his solo record. The saddest news for the killer, however, was discovering that the record company never reported the tapes missing. The conclusion he had come to was that nobody cared enough about them or what was on the tapes.

As the first song began to play back over the Advent studio speakers, the murderer's mind began to drift back, way back to a time when the whole world was in front of him and anything was possible with the music and the band he had created. *We had everything with Marty, Anthony, Jimmy and me. The first single was a very small success. But the record was going to be big. REAL BIG. I had the concept all laid out. The band was in the zone. So why did that loser Peterson have to do that to us? He had his thing going—why couldn't he just help us out? And why didn't my mates rescue me? They knew my screw up was just a temporary setback. IT WAS JUST A MATTER OF TIME!*

The killer picked up a recent music magazine and the contents inside only depressed him further. The article was entitled, "Second Time's A Charm." It was a feature story about all the reissues and reformatting of classic rock records from the Sixties. Naturally, the expanded *Everything Is Nothing* by The Winding Roads was one of the records they focused on. The reissue got rave reviews, which included numerous alternate takes, rough home demos by Peterson, and songs recorded but not included on the original record.

There was, of course, nothing re-released from the killer's former band because his record never saw the light of day—courtesy of Tommy Peterson. But he couldn't put out a CD anyway of his "lost classic" because he had stolen the reels—not that the label would even know what to do with them if they were anonymously returned. With many of the older rock legends wanting one more shot at the money, however, there were thousands of reissues every year. Sadly, his former band only had one, low-charting single and he and his band never got to the album that was supposed to be.

While the murderer continued to tinker around in the studio, he saw the red light blinking furiously. It was the front doorbell light. The killer had linked the doorbell to a red light so that he would know someone was there during a recording session. Since he never had any regular visitors to the house, he always ignored the doorbell. A couple of minutes went by and the red light stopped flashing. The visitor had apparently walked away.

As the fugitive walked to the back room to get something from the refrigerator, he could see a man walking around his property. All he could make out from the basement window was a pair of khaki pants and brown shoes. The killer didn't think it was a cop but the man wasn't checking the electric meters either. The murderer walked up the stairs and peered out a back window to get a better look at his face from the window. He looked very familiar but he couldn't make him out; the killer's eyes didn't work too well at far distances. But he definitely didn't want him snooping around for much longer. The nosy neighbors would end up calling and then he would get a visit from the police. He had no choice but to find out who this person was.

"Can I help you?' said the killer as he stuck his head out from behind the door.

"Hey, don't you recognize me? It's Johnny Merseburg. From *Rock Forever* magazine? We met at the memorial concert. How are you?"

The killer smiled politely as he knew who the trespasser was. But he was very confused. *Why was Johnny Merseburg coming out here unannounced? And why did I ever give this idiot my contact information the other night?*

"Listen, we were thinking of doing a big story on the Peterson memorial show and we want to do some features on those that participated. You were pretty good up there. May I come in? I'm sorry I came up on you so fast like this but I was in the area and I need to get this story real soon. My lead reporter is not around so I figured I'd do it. Nice place you have here." The nervous Merseburg was talking so fast the words were coming out of his mouth at blinding speed.

"Thank you," said the killer, "but I'm not really up for it right now. I don't feel too well."

"Oh, I'll be real quick," said Merseburg. "I promise."

The fugitive knew something wasn't right here. He knew Merseburg and his magazine but his timing for a visit was peculiar. The killer didn't want to seem paranoid but he was curious as to why he couldn't do this interview on the telephone. "Who was the reporter who was supposed to come out here?"

"Oh, a guy from way back—Tony Russo. That's not important. So can I just get a few questions from you?"

*Tony Russo? No, that's very important. The same Tony Russo I saw talking with the cops.* The killer knew right away that this was no coincidence. The publisher knew something about him and the Peterson murder case and the link between Russo and the cops. *Mr. Merseburg is not aware that I know exactly what his reporter Mr. Russo is up to these days. I can also see that he is packing a gun inside his jacket. He is onto me. Oh, that is unfortunate. Stay cool.*

The murderer turned back into his house as he spoke. "Yeah, why not? But let's do the interview in my basement-recording studio." The only way that the killer was going to get rid of Johnny Merseburg was to get him inside and off the street. He'd worry later about moving his car. It was becoming clear to the murderer that after he took care of the rock publisher, he had to leave town. It was only a matter of time before they would catch up to him.

"Uh, yeah. Why don't you show me the way?" said a very hyper Merseburg. The publisher assumed because the killer had met him the night before, there was no known threat and he was simply here to do a follow-up story. Merseburg believed all he had to do was get some answers onto his hidden cassette recorder and use his gun to keep the murderer at bay until the cops arrived. But he had to get the interview first. The story came first.

The wanted man led Merseburg through the living room and down the basement stairs, with the publisher following several steps behind. As they entered the basement recording studio, the killer was more than ready to hit a hidden light switch that would black out the entire basement instantly. Once that occurred, it would soon be the end of the road for Johnny Merseburg.

# CHAPTER 25

▼

Tony Russo held the faded publicity photograph that his rock critic friend Don Bart had given him from his files. This was the new face of evil—and a familiar one at that.

"It's Freddy Weiss…from, uh…"

"Black Manic Panic," said Bart. "Boy, Tony. You either have to start listening to some more classic rock tunes or reading a couple of rock encyclopedias."

"I remember. Sorry I didn't know it as fast as you," said Russo. "I saw Freddy at Peterson's memorial concert. But I only know a little bit about him and nothing about that band you just mentioned. I know Freddy from that solo record in the Seventies. He had one song that got around a bit."

"Ah, see? You're not as slow as you appear," said Bart. "So many people know the singer Van Morrison but they always forget about his band Them, the band that Van started out with from '64 to '66. Anyway, the Seventies song of Freddy's was

205

"Taking A Walk" and some company used it in their underarm deodorant commercial. You know, people walking into town, walking on the beach, walking to work. I'm guessing Weiss got a cut every time it aired and it paid the bills. For a short time, I guess."

"What's the story on him? And what's the connection to Peterson?"

Bart sat down on the couch and swung his long legs up onto his glass table. "Well, from what I remember was that Freddy Weiss was a Brit and came over and became the founder and singer of a US-based band called Black Manic Panic. They cut a single and were getting ready to release some sort of big rock musical as their debut called *Timelessness*. The word on the street was that Weiss' concept was somewhat similar to what Peterson and The Winding Roads were doing and a bit better than Tommy's."

"Huh. Not much different than The Beatles' *Sgt. Pepper's* and The Beach Boys' *Smile* concept album race," said Russo.

"Well, sort of," said Bart. "But we know how that turned out. In any period of music, there's always competition or a race for the same fans and critics. And the window on how creative you can get while trying to sell records does open and shut rather fast. And The Beatles got theirs done while The Beach Boys had issues with Brian Wilson. Anyway, getting back to what I was saying, Weiss and Peterson were friends for a short period of time over in London and met up again when Weiss arrived in New York City. They were very aware as to what the other one was doing."

"Interesting. I never heard any of this from Tommy," said Russo.

"Now remember that Weiss was the only Brit while the other three members of BMP were US citizens," said Bart. "Weiss flew back to London because they were having problems getting the record done and he wanted to get his head together. But Weiss got busted for drugs in a raid. Back then, you know that was a tougher rap to beat than today. Because of his arrest, The Roads and their management didn't want them on the US tour. The UK wouldn't give Weiss a work visa to tour the US. Like what happened to the Kinks' visa problems in the late Sixties, it was an issue if you couldn't tour the States. I know Indigo was with Peterson by now and she was 'making decisions' in terms of telling Tommy what he should do and started up all sorts of negative vibes about Freddy. The bottom line was no one wanted to have Weiss and BMP and their new record competing with Peterson's concept. So nobody pulled any favors to help Freddy out."

"So Weiss couldn't get back to the States to tour with BMP or finish the project," said Russo.

"You got it. The Roads just walked away from Freddy. But he dug his own grave, Tony. He got busted so who's fault was that? Now the other three US members of BMP got tired of waiting for this thing to be resolved. I know they weren't enamored of Freddy's concept anyway so they ditched Weiss and tried to form a new band. And as you might expect, without a leader, they fell apart a few months later."

"So Peterson and Indigo conspired to get Weiss and his band out of the way," said Russo.

"Well, that's a bit dramatic," said Bart. "Look, it's been well documented that Tommy was paranoid about a lot of things. You know that. If a rumor was going around that BMP's inter-active musical could surpass The Winding Roads' effort, my guess is Indigo and Tommy saw an opportunity to beat them to the punch," said Bart. "But there's probably a bunch of other stories about Tommy that you don't know about. You know it was a crazy time, Tony. Some people and their careers got caught in the crossfire."

For three decades, Russo had been as close to Tommy Peterson as any other rock critic could be. He thought that the two of them had developed a special relationship by sharing many personal stories and experiences. But in the end, Russo felt somewhat betrayed that he knew nothing about Freddy Weiss. The fact that Bart knew this story and Russo didn't at all left a bitter taste in his mouth. *What was the point of working on Tommy's autobiography if he wasn't going to give me all the information?* thought Russo.

But it was all starting to make sense. Russo believed Weiss had timed his revenge with the 35th anniversary award that Peterson was going to receive for *Everything Is Nothing*—the record that may *NOT* have been a success if BMP's *Timelessness* had been released. *Weiss*, thought Russo, *probably felt it should have been him receiving that outstanding musical achievement award.* The evidence around the crime scenes was proof enough that all of the killings had absolutely nothing to do about money. It was all about revenge.

But where was Freddy Weiss?

"Well, thanks for the history lesson, Don," said Russo as he stood up quickly to shake Bart's hand.

"That's it? I had you scheduled here for almost another hour," said Bart.

"Yeah, I'm sorry. But I'm very behind on this book and my article for the magazine," said Russo.

"That's a strange bird you're working for, that Merseburg character. Quite a brawler I heard back in his playboy days," said Bart as he pulled Russo's jacket out from the hall closet. "His magazine's so-so. I don't think they've quite found their editorial voice yet. You know what I mean?"

Russo's mind was running wild. He wasn't even listening to what Bart was saying. He had to get out of his friend's apartment right away, run down to his car and figure out what his plan of action would be. For Russo, everything was pointing directly to Weiss: the Englishman who left an English boot print found at the murder scenes, the memorial concert that Weiss performed at and later murdered Indigo, the fact that Peterson dropped his friend Weiss and his band Black Manic Panic off their US tour. The facts were all there.

"Yeah, ok. Well, I'll give you a buzz and we'll do lunch soon," said Russo as he scampered down to the elevator. Bart shook his head in amazement as he watched his former rival leave the apartment.

*Who do I have to call first? Caitlin? I don't remember her cell phone number,"* said Russo to himself as he jumped into his car. *Wait. Call the office and get Ed on the phone.* Russo dialed his new intern's number as he drove erratically across the Brooklyn Bridge. Ed Mooney picked up after the second ring.

"Ed Mooney."

"Ed, Tony Russo. How are ya, buddy?"

"I am doing well. And yourself?"

"Listen, is Susan Barkin at her desk?" asked Russo.

It was quiet on the phone line for a second as Mooney checked.

"Nope," said Rooney.

Russo knew that like many young interns, they were easily tricked into doing just about anything if you phrased it the right way. "Ed, Johnny called me earlier and said that if I needed to get Freddy Weiss' address, just have someone dig it out from his Rolodex. So you're the guy today."

"Really? Um, shouldn't Susan do that?"

The intern was not responding fast enough to Russo's request. "She's not there, I'm on the road, so I need you to do this quickly," said Russo.

"Ok. Hold on," said Mooney as he put Russo on hold.

Russo waited on the phone for Mooney in what seemed like an eternity. If Barkin came back, Russo knew she wouldn't give him that information because she would know Russo was lying. The phone clicked and Mooney was back on the line with Russo.

"Tony, I'm at Johnny's desk. That's really weird..."

"What's weird? Just give me the address, Ed. I'm in a real rush," said Russo.

"Sorry," said Mooney. "It's 7428 Nassau Boulevard. The phone number is..."

"I don't need a phone number. Thanks for getting it so quick."

"Tony, it was open right to his name. I didn't have to look for it. That's what I thought was so weird."

Russo lowered the cell phone from his hand. Merseburg had already beaten him to the punch. The classic rock fan-turned-publisher was one smart cookie. Russo came to the realization that he had accidentally spilled the beans to his boss by calling into Ed Mooney earlier. Now Merseburg was out there playing investigative reporter, knowing full well that Freddy Weiss was the prime suspect in three murders. But it was Russo's own fault for not thinking ahead. He was not a detective and did not have the luxury of having someone nearby like Caitlin O'Connell to tell him how *not* to give up a possible suspect's name to a civilian.

"So Johnny's not there in the office, is he?" said Russo.

"Nope," said Mooney. "He left about a half hour ago. And I don't think he's too happy with you. Neither is Susan." Just what Russo needed to hear—an intern giving him some perspective about his job future.

"Ed, get out of Johnny's office and go back to your desk. I'll talk to you later. And don't tell them I called."

Russo hung up the phone and began to scratch the sides of his head furiously. Merseburg was not answering his cell phone and he couldn't find O'Connell's cell phone number. But Russo, feeling a sense of responsibility for his boss, needed to prevent Johnny Merseburg from doing something asinine like visiting Freddy Weiss by himself. Weiss was a killer and Merseburg was heading for a heap of trouble.

If Russo called the cops, they would want to know why a music reporter was playing detective and withholding critical information on a big homicide case. Knowing Merseburg never stepped foot on Long Island, Russo could intercept him while waiting for O'Connell's call. She was already on Long Island and he could tell the detective what he discovered about Freddy Weiss and what to do next.

It sounded like a rational plan at the time. Russo placed his cell phone back on his lap as drove towards Garden City. His detective friend would be calling him any minute now.

# CHAPTER 26

▼

Caitlin O'Connell was driving back west on the Long Island Expressway from her meeting with Tommy Peterson's ex-manager Ryan Guttridge. Tony Russo had his reservations about how her meeting might go with Guttridge, but the meeting went better than she expected. But what the detective didn't return with was a name, someone she could link to the Peterson murder cases. O'Connell had promised herself and Chief Consoli that in a few days, she'd at least have a couple of credible names they could investigate. But Guttridge's damaged memory banks were unable to produce a single name.

The detective looked down at her sports watch. O'Connell had not heard from Tony Russo in a few hours. She was hoping that perhaps he would be luckier in getting some answers from his old reporter rival, Don Bart. Although Russo wasn't trained in how to ascertain information from experts during a homicide case, O'Connell was counting on Russo's veteran reporter skills in getting a name or two for the police department.

Her cell phone suddenly began to vibrate. O'Connell rolled up her window as she fumbled to put her hands-free earpiece into her ear. But the number was unfamiliar. It wasn't Tony.

"O'Connell here."

"Caitlin, it's Pete from the M.E.'s office."

Pete O'Hanlon was an old neighborhood friend of O'Connell's who worked in the medical examiner's office. O'Hanlon, like so many others in their neighborhood, carried on a family tradition by following in his dad's profession. But O'Hanlon never forgot about the families they had grown up with and their two families happened to be tight. Any time an autopsy was being performed on a case that O'Connell was involved with, O'Hanlon was usually the first to call his detective friend.

"Hey Pete. How are ya? Whaddya got for me?" said O'Connell.

"About Tommy Peterson? We have some more to do but it seems he had a major fall before he was murdered," said O'Hanlon. "There was trauma to the forehead from a hard fall. We got in touch with his doctor and he said that Peterson suffered from Meniere's disease. Loud noises really affected him."

O'Connell remembered seeing traces of blood on the floor a few feet from the chair that Peterson was murdered in. "So that meant Peterson first fell out of the chair he was found in, passing out from the high volume?"

"Looks that way," said O'Hanlon. "We're assuming he wasn't tied down to the seat as well as he should have been when the music got cranking in the studio. But we checked his ears more carefully and we did find traces of foam in each of his ears. But no ear plugs belonging to the victim were found. That's the only thing that would have saved him."

"No, that's not right, Pete," said O'Connell. "Can't be. We found ear plugs at the scene on the studio floor right next to Peterson."

As O'Connell held the phone, a beeping noise was coming through her cell phone. The message icon was blinking. The detective had a new message on her voice mail but it would have to wait until she was finished with O'Hanlon.

"Hey Pete, I just got a phone message. We gotta hurry this up," said O'Connell.

"I know you found earplugs," said O'Hanlon. "It's in the report. But the traces of foam we found inside of Peterson's ears were tan-colored. I'm guessing to match his ear? But the ones on the floor you found, however, were green. They were some-one else's earplugs, Caitlin. Not Peterson's."

O'Connell was stunned by what her old neighborhood buddy had just told her. The killer left a pair of earplugs behind after he was finished murdering Tommy Peterson?

"Did you have any luck picking up traces of anything from those earplugs?" inquired O'Connell.

"You know, Caitlin. Sometimes we get a bit lucky. We actually got a microscopic drop of dried blood on one of those green earplugs that don't match Peterson's. So we have our DNA sample on the suspect," said O'Hanlon.

"Incredible. Absolutely incredible. You guys are like magicians," said the detective.

"Think so?" said O'Hanlon. "Then you'll really like this. Those green earplugs had small letters on them."

"Letters? On earplugs? You mean L for left and R for right?" said O'Connell.

O'Hanlon burst out laughing. "No, not L and R. It's three letters on each earplugs—BMP. Maybe it's the manufacturer?"

*Or the killer's initials*, thought O'Connell. "Pete, thanks a million. But I have to grab this other message. I'll talk to ya later."

As O'Connell hung up with O'Hanlon, she wondered who could possibly have the initials BMP. She rifled through her long alphabetical lists laying in her lap that had all the names Russo had mentioned to her. But she could not find anyone with the initials BMP or even BP. O'Connell knew that it had to be someone that they had accidentally missed. The detective then dialed into her voice message box to retrieve the one message that was waiting for her.

This one was from Tony Russo.

"Caitlin, where are you?" said a frantic Russo on the message. "I couldn't find your number and you haven't called me all day. Listen, I think I know who the killer is. It's a guy Peterson knew years ago. His name is Freddy Weiss and Peterson and Indigo screwed him out of some big tour many years ago back in the late Sixties. And Weiss was at the memorial concert and performed. But I screwed up, Caitlin, 'cause my publisher Johnny got wind that I was looking for Weiss and I think he went over to get the story on his own at Freddy's' house. I didn't call the cops but I'm calling you. I'm heading over to Garden City now to see if I can get there before he does. Meet me over there and call me back soon!"

*You idiot!* O'Connell yelled to herself as the message ended. *Why are you doing that, Tony? And what is the address?* O'Connell's warnings by Chief Consoli about getting a civilian like Russo involved in a homicide investigation was ringing in her ears. O'Connell knew she was only about twenty minutes away from Garden City but the detective had to call information and find out where Weiss' house was located immediately. Before she could dial the number, however, O'Connell's phone rang again.

"Tony?" yelled O'Connell.

"No, this is Ryan Guttridge. I wanted…"

"Ryan, wait a second. Does the name Freddy Weiss mean anything to you?" said O'Connell.

"Freddy Weiss…Freddy—oh yeah," said Guttridge. "I remember Freddy. Angry little British prick back in the Sixties. Thought he was the next 'big thing' in the rock world way back when. Didn't they all?"

"And what about BMP? Does that ring a bell?" asked O'Connell.

"BMP? Yeah. Black Manic Panic," said Guttridge. "That was Freddy's band back then. What of it?"

*BMP. The initials on the green earplugs,* thought O'Connell. Russo had told her about a bunch of old rockers taking out green earplugs at the memorial concert during an interview after 'someone' backstage had been giving them out.

"Freddy was an English guy who brought some guys from the States together to make BMP. Come to think of it, you know Freddy and Tommy knew each other…"

O'Connell hung up on Guttridge in mid-sentence, threw her red light up on her car as she dialed a different number other than Russo's. An unfamiliar man's voice answered.

"Garden City police. Sergeant Figliozzi. How can I help you?"

# CHAPTER 27

▼

Tony Russo was now standing outside the screen door to Freddy Weiss' colonial-style house. Recognizing Johnny Merseburg's obnoxious looking, mid-Seventies black and gold Trans Am, Russo knew his publisher had foolishly followed through on Russo's accidental tip he had given to intern Ed Mooney. He didn't know why Merseburg would do such a ridiculous thing but Russo needed to ask himself the same question. Why was HE here?

Glancing down at his cell phone, there was still no message from Detective O'Connell. Russo wasn't sure that he had made the best purchase when it came to his cell phone. He could never get a clear signal, the phone's buttons kept sticking, his voice mail messages would sometimes arrive later rather than a minute later and the little gray antenna was starting to come loose. But it was all he had.

Russo saw the front door was open slightly and knocked on it. No one responded. He knew Merseburg was around there somewhere but after calling out "Hello?" a few more times,

Russo cautiously stepped into the house and began to look around. With a minimal amount of furniture and newspapers throughout the living room, it looked as if the entire house hadn't been dusted or washed in eons. There was a Taylor acoustic guitar and a black Gibson electric guitar lying on the floor, with the Black Beauty model having sustained some extensive damage. As Russo proceeded towards the back of the main floor, he could see a bright red light glowing above the slightly opened basement door.

What was down those basement stairs made Russo nervous but also very curious. Before entering the basement, however, Russo looked to his right, spotting a large knife on the counter and a wooden broom propped up in the corner of the kitchen. He grabbed both and walked down the stairs slowly. As Russo reached the landing, he turned and stepped through the beads hanging from the doorframe.

Upon first glance, the entire basement had been turned into a creepy-looking rock and roll museum about the Sixties. More importantly, it was an over-the-top shrine to Weiss and his former band. There were tons of posters and pictures of Black Manic Panic sandwiched in between the great rockers of the decade: Janis Joplin singing at Monterey, Freddy Weiss on the beach, Jim Morrison backstage, a Black Manic Panic publicity shot, Bob Dylan in the studio, Freddy Weiss in a bathtub. There were thousands of sheets of lyrics and music taped up against the wall. Old Nehru jackets and fringe vests hung from the ceiling. Lava lamps and tie-dyed blankets were scattered all throughout the cluttered basement.

In the middle of the basement was a working recording studio, complete with a recording console positioned in front of a large window that was dark, otherwise known as the "live" room. It was an isolated room where a band came in to set up their equipment and record their tracks without outside noise creeping in during the session. From Russo's perspective, nothing was "live" in this house. This was a world that had died decades ago.

"I hope you're not looking for Johnny," said a voice from behind the hanging beads. "And I certainly hope you're not looking for me."

Russo started to shake as Freddy Weiss stepped through the hanging beads. It was only a few days ago when the two spoke briefly at the Tommy Peterson memorial concert but the situation was much different now. No one had managed to uncover who the killer was until today. And Freddy Weiss was looking to keep it that way. Permanently.

"Don't even think of trying anything, Freddy. I have a knife and a club in my hand," said Russo. As a journalist, he was the furthest thing from a street fighter but he wasn't about to give in.

"Tony, I will kill you this very second unless you put those things down right now," said Weiss as he displayed a large black .357 Magnum. "I have killed four people already. Don't be number five."

After briefly thinking about hurling the knife at Weiss, in the back of his head he knew O'Connell had probably gotten his message and was on her way with the rest of the NYPD to save him from this maniac. He dropped both of them at his side.

"Four?"

"Your idiot boss is permanently resting in my back room," said Weiss. "I really don't know what would possess fools like you or him to come down here. I mean, what did you think you were going to do after you walked in here?"

Russo said, "I assumed Johnny was in trouble and…"

Weiss cut him off. "You're right about the trouble part. And there's your problem. You assumed. Remember that old Odd Couple TV episode when Felix tells Oscar that when you ASSUME you make an *ass* of *u* and *me*? You wouldn't be staring down the barrel of a gun now if you thought a bit more clearly. Right?"

Russo said nothing.

"RIGHT? ANSWER THE QUESTION!" yelled Weiss.

"Right," said Russo quietly.

As Russo stood at attention, in the back of his mind, he was begging for his detective friend Caitlin to show up now more than anything in the world. Russo just wanted to be back in his house with his wife and kids and nothing more. It was a stupid thing to come to a possible suspect's house. *Why didn't I just call the cops and explain the situation after they arrested Weiss?* thought Russo. The rock journalist had no choice now but to stall for time.

Weiss switched on the bright lights to the main room as well as the lights in the live room. Russo could see a giant black recliner surrounded by a circle of large amplifiers. It looked frighteningly familiar to how they had found Tommy Peterson in his home studio.

"What do you want from me?" said Russo.

"Shut up and take a seat in that room," replied Weiss. "Now."

With Weiss trailing behind Russo, they entered the adjoining room. The killer directed Russo to slide his body into the black recliner. The handcuffs attached to the sides and the end of the recliner was not a comforting sight for the journalist.

"If I had to kidnap Tommy, this is where he would have been," said Weiss. "But after reading an article that Tommy had a ton of amps at his studio, well, I decided that it was easier to kill him there than try and drag him back from Manhattan. Now put those handcuffs on by yourself. Feet first, then the right hand. I'll be able to hear if they're locked."

Russo moved slowly but did as he was told. As the rock critic scanned the room looking for a possible way out, he noticed the various posters that covering the studio walls. They were happened to be from the James Bond movie series.

"I see you've been admiring my interior decorating, Tony," said Weiss as he locked the last handcuff into place. "I was a big fan of those movies in the Sixties and I've never tired of them. Great British flicks, those Bond productions. Although I don't have the high-tech abilities of those fictional mastermind criminals, I do have a plan."

"Freddy, I don't understand why you have to…"

"Damn. I knew I forgot something," said Weiss. The killer reached down to the floor and picked up a roll of gray duct tape. Walking behind the recliner, he taped up Russo's mouth quickly.

"Tony, it's bad enough I had to read your endless crap. So I really don't want to hear your comments," said Weiss. "I'd rather you listen to me. It's more important, don't you think?"

Overcome by emotion, Russo began to cry as he thrashed about in the recliner. There still was no sign of Detective O'Connell and time was clearly running out for the rock journalist.

"Now, now, you just have to relax," said Weiss. "I won't be pushing a guitar through your body like I did to dear old Tommy. I remembered that Flying V guitar on one of his promo shots from the *Everything Is Nothing* record. So I thought it was a nice sendoff by GIVING IT TO HIM with his own precious guitar. It certainly made the whole scene a bit more dramatic, don't you think?"

Russo lay there, unable to move or communicate. He knew something terrible was going to happen to him, but he wasn't sure what Weiss had in mind. Russo had his opportunity to attack Weiss when he had a knife and a broom but it would have been no match for his gun. All he could do was pray for Caitlin.

Weiss strolled back into the main room and returned with a small chair to sit just a few feet away from Russo.

"It's time for a little Rock History 101," said Weiss. "Tony, do you know what this is?" He held up a sketch for an album cover. Russo stared at him with a blank stare.

"No ideas? No recollections? Well, I'm not surprised you don't know. No one knows. It's a test cover of what was supposed to be Black Manic Panic's finest hour: the *Timelessness* record. We used this cover on some of the promo demos for our record label execs. As you can see, it's a drawing of a circle of different sized amplifiers aimed out showing the high volume pumping out from the amps. And in the center is us! You may notice that the sketch was similar in design to the Stonehenge ruins."

*Stonehenge. The murder scene was set up just like the famous ancient ruins,* thought Russo. *There were photos of Stonehenge on the floor of Tommy's studio.*

"It was bad enough when Tommy decided to boot us off their US tour as the opening act. But that stupid girlfriend of his, Indigo, started a joke that our songs probably sounded as old and broken as Stonehenge. The record company, who originally liked the cover, suddenly turned on us. After a couple of meetings about doing a full record, the record company said 'Freddy, I don't think we can't use this.' And my band mates, who understood nothing about my vision, just waited and waited for me to get back from London. But I couldn't 'cause I got busted! I had to try and defend the project all by myself while I was locked up!"

Russo was listening but all he could think about was where his detective friend was. Weiss was slowly starting to come apart at the seams and the rock journalist didn't want to be here when he exploded.

"My career went in the toilet and Tommy Peterson was the one I hold responsible. After I got out of jail, I spent weeks and months trying to get the record company interested again in doing this record but no one wanted to go near me. My band mates weren't around anymore, so I was working on trying to rework and re-record every track. My wife left me in the process. Said she didn't understand the politics of music and didn't care. All she wanted to know was where the money was. The label dropped me and I was history."

Weiss reached up and took out his only solo album, the independent record that he put out in the early Seventies. The killer had taken the Stonehenge sketch for his aborted record with BMP and instead used it for the cover of his solo effort. It was clear to Russo, and anyone else, that the amateurish painting could not have helped in selling the indie release.

"I find it somewhat amusing that you gave this a bad review," said Weiss as he held the record up in the air. Russo didn't remember writing the scathing review of Weiss' self-released record *Phaedrus*. He had done so many reviews that it was hard to keep track.

"One thing you should always remember, Tony. Aggression unchallenged is aggression unleashed. Sound familiar?"

That expression Russo remembered—*it was the quote that was on the piece of paper that had been left on Tommy Peterson's body.*

"It came from the Roman fables writer Phaedrus. I think the quote fits me and my record quite well, don't you think? At least I think I know what it means. It doesn't matter. What does matter was I wasn't going to sit around anymore and watch Tommy grab any more money or headlines that should have been mine to begin with. As for this record, the fact I got any press back then from a small indie record I thought was impressive. Instead, everybody decided to take one more cheap shot at me. You know, have a little fun at the washed-up rocker's expense. But I was a scrappy guy, Tony. I got some business hack interested in a song off this record and got me back on my feet."

The ex-musician killer pulled up an old Marshall guitar amplifier head and stood up over Russo as he continued. "But by '73, man, I was done. And I tried everything to stay in rock and roll. Everything and anything I could think of. In the late Seventies I opened up a punk clothing store but every other kid would try to shoplift something out. In the early Eighties, I went into music video producing but once those big ass entertainment companies squeezed out us independents, I was toast in just a couple of years. I even tried managing a couple of alternative bands in the Nineties but they wanted no part of a 'nobody' like me." Weiss began to rub his face back and forth. The stress was coming back.

"And every year I struggled, I kept reading about how much money The Winding Roads had made. All of the things THEY had I could have had if they just opened their minds and let us go on tour with them back in '69. There was plenty of money to go around for everyone. But not Tommy. Not Indigo. They knew what I was capable of and they chose to abandon me. And when I would bump into them at a festival many years later, it was all smiles as if they had no recollection of what they had done. Nothing. It was amazing. But when I started reading last year about the upcoming 35th anniversary of *Everything Is Nothing*, there was never a mention of my project or me. Know why? 'Cause I didn't exist in popular music anymore."

Weiss was now only inches away from Russo's face as the killer pushed a pair of green earplugs into his own ears. "That's why those detailed rock history books by Elvis, The Beatles, Bob Dylan and the rest do so well. PEOPLE FORGET. In the end, well, there was only one thing for me to do. I wanted to make sure no one would forget what happened to Tommy Peterson. And when the moment was right, when I had all the information that I needed about where Tommy was, I would stomp on him like the little insect that he was."

Russo looked at Weiss and then closed his eyes. He could not listen to this madman any longer.

"Tony," said Weiss. "I know it's over for me. I doubt I'll be able to run from the law much longer, especially knowing you're here and Johnny's rotting away in the back room. 'Cause I know you've been hanging around that cop—you were working with them, weren't you?"

The rock critic shook his head back and forth in denial.

"C'mon, Tony. I saw you at Tommy's wake talking to that O'Connell cop," said Weiss. "And Merseburg gave you up as well. He wouldn't have ended up here if you hadn't been playing cop, right? You and that O'Connell girl! Some team! You're the one confronting the killer and she's out somewhere looking for clues! Priceless."

Russo was starting to arch his back in a feeble attempt to get out of the recliner. The reality was starting to set in that perhaps his new detective friend was not going to rescue him in time.

"What I am going to do now," said Weiss, "is give you a first-hand peek at what the rock world missed back in '69. As you have learned, I've been a big fan of the James Bond movies. So I have made my own devious device down here. Courtesy of all these very lovely speakers I have placed around the room, I will slowly increase the music from inside the other room. And by the time I'm through with you, Tony, my music will be the last thing you'll ever hear on Earth."

Weiss hopped off his chair and closed the soundproofed studio door behind him. Russo started to count how many speakers were in the room: twelve. The rock critic wasn't a sound expert, but each one of the cabinets looked like they could easily generate a ton of power. Russo's doctor had warned him a few years ago that if he attended future rock shows, he had to start wearing earplugs to protect what was left of his hearing. This time, however, there were no earplugs around. Even if Russo happened to survive this madman's ordeal, he would be stone cold deaf by the time help arrived.

With his music reel already in place, Weiss pressed PLAY on the control module. In a few seconds, Russo could hear the volume rising slowly through the bank of speakers. The classic rock music sounds of Black Manic Panic were now seeping through the speakers loud and clear in the live room as Russo continued to squirm in his seat. The pain that was deep inside his ears was starting to come back. Suddenly, the sound went off and Weiss' voice came through the overhead speaker.

"In case you were wondering, Tony, I was only at 4 out of a possible 10. Pretty impressive, huh? So sit back and enjoy. As Nigel Tufnel once said in that *Spinal Tap* movie, 'This one goes to eleven,'" said Weiss.

Russo began to pray as the sound began to rise again from the speakers. Not to God but to a very, very good detective friend of his that was very, very late.

# CHAPTER 28

▼

"Listen, I've got a ton of detectives working this case. I've got patrolmen posting up signs and asking questions in the area. AND I've got a ton of volunteers who are asking how they can be of assistance. Don't forget all the psychics and the profilers who want time with us. So I've got nothing else to say other than we are doing everything we can. I gotta go."

Chief John Consoli hung up on the reporter. Normally, he wouldn't have taken a call like this but it had come from a retired cop friend of his. The ex-cop was working as a special crime correspondent for a cable news network. The chief's old buddy was now making a nice secondary income on top of his 30-year pension. Consoli himself was nearing that mark this year and he was going to follow exactly what his buddy had done: cash in and get out.

But for now, the embattled chief was under all sorts of heat from everyone in New York City. Three murders in just a few days and all linked together via a couple of footprints from a rare English boot. There was the backstage show ID tag that the killer may have left behind but there was no name to go with it. The word was getting around that there was a connection to the killer and the music industry but they weren't 100% positive. And his lead detective on this case, Detective Caitlin O'Connell, had not stayed in touch today. For her not to call in on a case of this magnitude was unusual.

"Has anyone heard from O'Connell?" yelled Consoli to a number of detectives in the squad room.

"No," said Detective Ed Suarez, "not yet. But Chief, I did some follow up with this older lady at a music store that…"

"Well someone find out where she is. What about her buddy, Ed? Where is Glover?" said Consoli.

"Steve's off today. Chief, listen to me. I think this might be worth taking a second look at," said Suarez as he followed the annoyed Consoli into his office.

"Make it quick. I have to meet with the deputy commissioner in 15 minutes," said Consoli as he reached for the bottle of aspirin inside his desk.

"You told us to start keeping an eye on any unusual police-related activity related to music—stores, concerts, shops, anything," said Suarez.

"Yeah?"

"Well, the other day I read about a Tower Records store being vandalized."

"So a kid threw a brick through their window," said Consoli. "So what?"

Suarez shook his head. "No, nothing like that. This happened during regular business hours. Some older guy was causing all kinds of havoc in a music store and threatened one of the employees."

"Ok. The manager got pissed and they tossed him, right?"

"No. What I thought was interesting was the guy was in the book section of the store. Apparently an eyewitness said he got crazy while he was reading this book and started ripping a page out of a book and that's when the whole thing started."

Consoli looked at his watch. The pressure was on his department to find out who was responsible for these murders, but he wasn't hearing anything right now from Detective Suarez that made this story worth his time. Suarez was a good detective but he wasn't known for breaking cases, so Consoli wasn't exactly sure what to make of his analysis.

"What's the tie-in, Ed?" said Consoli as he stared out the window.

"The eyewitness said he was an older gentleman rambling on about how everyone in the store should know who he was. And the book he damaged was—get this—a book about The Winding Roads," said Suarez.

Consoli turned around and looked directly at Suarez.

"A Winding Roads book? You're kidding," said Consoli.

"Not at all, Chief," said Suarez. "He was reading something and the guy apparently went nuts. White guy, older guy, possible musician guy…"

"What was on the page?" said the chief.

"Well, we don't know yet. I…"

"Oh, for Pete's sake, Ed. Is someone looking into this for you?" said Consoli.

"Yes! One of the women at the bookstore is looking into it for me today. Should be getting…"

"Suarez! Line 3! Some lady from Tower Records?" yelled someone from inside the squad room.

"Ed, pick it up in here," said Consoli. For the first time in days, Consoli was excited about a possible lead in the murder cases. Suarez turned on the speakerphone.

"Hello?" said a husky-sounding woman.

"Detective Suarez here, ma'am. What do you have for us? Who are we speaking with?"

"My name is Ann Hoffman. I'm the store manager."

"I spoke with you earlier about the details. Do you know which page that was ripped?" asked Suarez.

"Yes I do. I have a new copy of the book. It was page 63. It is an oversized picture of Tommy Peterson with...wow, I don't believe it."

There was no sound on the other end of the receiver. The store manager was reading the caption to the photo but was only reading it to herself. Neither one of the detectives could hear what she was mumbling about. Consoli jumped in front of Suarez and yelled into the speaker.

"Ma'am, Chief Consoli here! What is on the page you're looking at?"

"That crazy guy that was in here the other day?" said Hoffman. "That ripped this book and threatened my staff? This is him! In the photo! The British guy! He just looks...younger. It's a picture of him standing right next to Tommy Peterson."

Consoli ran out of the room, yelling, "Someone get me O'Connell on the phone right now!" The chief wanted to know where his lead detective was on this case. He ran back into the room where Suarez was still speaking to the store manager.

"Ma'am, rip that entire picture out and fax it over to us at this number," interrupted Consoli. "And please do not discuss this with anyone until we arrive. What is the other guy's na…"

"You want me to rip out another photo? Are you kidding me? This is the only good book I have left," said Hoffman.

The detectives had forgotten that the store manager had no idea that they were investigating a triple murder and *not* a random vandalism case. But none of that mattered. They needed a name to go with that photo.

"Ma'am, just cooperate with us," barked Consoli. "Or we'll drive over and take it!"

"You're going to bring a squad car all the way over to Franklin Square in Nassau County? I'll fax the photo over to you right now. Give me a second," she said.

"Franklin Square…Long Island?" said Consoli to Suarez. The chief assumed it was a Tower Records store somewhere in Manhattan. That was where all the murders had been committed.

"Yeah," said Suarez. "Nassau County. I read it in Newsday, the Long Island newspaper."

"I'll be damned. He's not even from around here," said Consoli.

"Who's not around from here?" interrupted Hoffman. The detectives had forgotten she was listening on the other end of the phone.

"I'm sorry, Ms. Hoffman. We are sending a car out to you to ask some additional questions so you can give us a better description of the man," said Suarez. "But what's the guy's name in...?"

Before the store manager could answer, the fax machine was pushing through the picture they had asked for. Consoli and Suarez began to read the caption as it inched through the machine:

*Tommy Peterson (l) and Freddy Weiss of Black Manic Panic*

*at a recording studio in West London, Summer 1968*

"I had one of my store clerks scan it first and then fax it over to you. This way I won't ruin another book. So what are you going to do about this creep?" said Hoffman.

*Plenty*, thought Consoli. The detectives thanked the manager and hung up with her without going into details. It was time to call a quick meeting in the squad room. In a minute from now, Freddy Weiss would soon be the most wanted man in the New York metropolitan area.

# CHAPTER 29

▼

Turning her red police light off a block away, Detective Caitlin O'Connell had pulled her unmarked car a couple of houses away from Freddy Weiss' place. She could see three cars near his house: one was in the driveway and the two were parked in front. Although her first instinct was to contact the Garden City police, after the sergeant picked up the phone, O'Connell hung up before she spoke.

O'Connell had not heard from Tony Russo and had to assume he went in there looking for Johnny Merseburg. She feared Russo and Merseburg might be in danger if there was even a whiff of police presence near Weiss' house. Instead, she called her detective buddy Steve Glover on his weekday off to meet her around the corner; they would scope out the house together. Without fail, Glover was standing on the corner in plain clothes when she arrived.

As the detective stepped out of the car, O'Connell had been thinking so much about Russo that she had temporarily forgotten about how publisher Johnny Merseburg. Russo had told

O'Connell earlier that his foolhardy boss had a reputation for taking matters into his own hands. Knowing that a triple homicide suspect was inside, O'Connell was convinced that Merseburg, like Russo, had gotten in way over his head.

With the front door to Weiss' house wide open, the two NYPD detectives peered into the killer's house with guns close at their side, well aware that Weiss could ambush them at any time.

"Steve, wait up here by the front door while I go in," said O'Connell as he turned off her two-way radio.

"Caitlin, I think we should call for backup. This is crazy going in here like this," said Glover.

The music was blasting from beneath the main floor so if everyone was downstairs, no one was going to answer the front door. "Well someone's downstairs. Stay here and if you hear gunfire, then call for backup and come get me," said O'Connell.

"Great. That sounds like a real good plan," said Glover sarcastically. He knew O'Connell was going in no matter what he said.

Ignoring his snide comments, O'Connell headed for the downstairs door. A red light was beaming bright as the basement door was already open. The light meant a recording session was in session and visitors were not allowed to enter until the light went off. In this case, however, red meant green; it was time to go and find out what was happening. As the detective proceeded down the basement stairs, the music she heard coming from the basement wasn't anything familiar. It was sort of an odd mix between early Genesis and The Eagles but not at their professional levels.

Halfway down the stairs, the music suddenly stopped. Had someone heard her coming down? O'Connell had her finger paused on the trigger of her 9mm gun. Instead, she heard a booming, unfamiliar voice coming from a speaker.

"Relax, my friend, the next track is even better." In a second, the voice disappeared and the music was again roaring through the basement. So loud, in fact, that O'Connell thought she was front row center at a Madison Square Garden KISS concert. As she approached the bottom of the stairs, to the right were hanging beads in front of a closed door with a window that had been blacked out. To the left, the detective could see light behind what appeared to be a hidden door.

O'Connell felt around the edges and found a door handle. As she opened the door, the detective was now in the other half of the basement. And lying in the middle of the floor was the dead body of Johnny Merseburg. He had apparently been shot at close range with his own gun that was left in his lap. The 'JM4' carved into the handle of the gun easily identified the former publisher. Pressing her hand against his neck, O'Connell surmised that Merseburg had only been dead a short time. But there was still no sign of Tony Russo. The detective continued around the other part of the basement, past the small light bulb shining above the washing machine and dryer and towards another door on the other side that separated the studio from the basement. Her buddy had to be somewhere in that room.

The hard-rocking music that continued to blast through the cellar was louder than ever. O'Connell found a tissue in her back pocket and stuck some small pieces in both of her ears. It would at least cut out some of the volume. The door, to her surprise, had a small window but had not been blacked out like the other one. The detective could now see everything that was going on inside the recording studio.

*     *     *     *

Freddy Weiss was wailing away on his black Steinberger through his vintage Orange amplifier and MXR distortion pedal, as his song played through the studio. Weiss was jumping around doing all sorts of rock theatrics: the Pete Townshend windmill strumming, the Angus Young head shaking. Weiss knew every single second to the rock songs he had recorded decades earlier and was jamming hard to one of his personal favorites:

> *The word on the street / Yeah, you're the one I have to meet*
> *Take your photo, touch your hand /*
> *There you are on my newsstand/*
> *Oh yeah*

"Man, I feel great, Tony? How are you feeling? You haven't been talking that much," said Weiss as he laughed into the studio microphone. "Why is that?"

Russo couldn't answer, as the duct tape was firmly over his mouth. When the music first started up, it was loud but nothing he couldn't handle. But as Weiss continued to raise the volume levels, Russo could feel the vibrations in every part of his body. But all he could do was sit and suffer. He had his fair share of loud gigs; those Motörhead shows had put his ears to the test. But never at such close range. The hearing problems that Russo had developed were now causing him agony beyond belief.

Weiss, however, was having a grand old time, drinking straight out of a dirty whiskey bottle. He had now opened the studio door between him and Russo so he could feel some of the sonic power that Russo was receiving only a couple of feet away from his ears. For Weiss, it was yet another 1969 flashback—the music was loud, the lights in the room were swirling around, and the mood was *groovy*. Weiss hadn't a single care in the world, unless you wanted to count the four bodies that Weiss had murdered in the past couple of weeks. All of the major events in his life revolved around rock and roll music. He lived and breathed it day and night and that's the way he thought it would be until the end. Freddy Weiss could not escape the music even if he wanted to. He couldn't exist without it.

The washed-up rocker continued to sing to his music even after the song had already ended. Weiss began to stagger and yell out bizarre one-liners like, "Who needs the money anyway?" "You can't take it with ya!" and "I am the winner!" Weiss was drunk and out of control.

That did not bode well for Tony Russo, who was fading fast. The sound was literally killing him.

\*      \*      \*      \*

With a break in the music between songs, Detective O'Connell saw her opportunity. With her gun drawn, she kicked open the studio door and yelled, "POLICE! DON'T MOVE!"

O'Connell was only audible for a second as the next song kicked in at full volume. Weiss spotted her instantly and jumped towards the other door. O'Connell fired a shot at Weiss but it missed wide. Weiss reached up and hit the master light switch again and both rooms were pitch black again except for a couple of faint red lava lamps glowing in the dark. Weiss reached into his pocket for his gun and fired several shots over in her direction.

Ducking for cover, O'Connell was not surprised that the killer had a gun and that a couple of shots had come awfully close; Weiss obviously could handle his weapon quite well. The detective wasn't sure, however, that her partner Steve Glover was able to hear the shots above the music. Unable to find her two-way radio that had fallen off her, she stayed low to the ground but couldn't stay there forever.

Weiss, meanwhile, had managed to crawl through to the other side of the basement during the gunfire in hopes of taking O'Connell out a different way. He wasn't trained like a NYPD detective, but the killer still had the added advantage of knowing every space within his own basement. In a crawl space located underneath the stairs, Weiss knew of a small opening in one of the panels. It would give him just enough room to fit his gun through and kill the sitting duck detective.

O'Connell maintained her position as she was in unfamiliar territory. She didn't hear Weiss run up the stairs so he was most likely somewhere downstairs, armed and dangerous. But where was he? The loud music was a major distraction but she wasn't going to risk moving towards the studio controls to try to turn the sound off in the darkness. The studio board had some lights emanating from it but it would be impossible to figure out which knob would kill the volume.

Moving himself closer to the wall, Weiss spotted O'Connell's shadow in the near distance through a small peephole. All the murderer needed to do now was move the panel ever so slightly and he would have a bullet inside the detective's head in less than a second. As Weiss dislodged the panel from the wall, the faint light bulb from the backroom managed to push a single beam of light through the wall and across the darkened music studio.

O'Connell instinctively wheeled her gun around towards the white light, firing four times straight into the studio wall with her semiautomatic, 9-millimeter gun. Instantly, Weiss' body flopped through the broken wall, his bloody hands dangling just inches above the studio floor. The madman was no match for a detective's instincts and it cost Freddy Weiss his life. But the late rocker had finally accomplished his goal. He had officially become a famous rock star. According to Detective O'Connell, maybe infamous was a much better choice of words.

O'Connell jumped up and scrambled back towards the door to turn the overhead lights on as the music was still cranking away. Heading back over to the mixing board, there were a million knobs to choose from. O'Connell, who had spent time in recording studios, had forgotten where the volume knob was. The detective was tempted to yank every electrical plug out from the wall when she discovered a large blue volume knob underneath a piece of paper. O'Connell spun the knob quickly to the left and the sound was off for good.

"Tony? Are you ok?" yelled O'Connell as she ran into the live room.

There was no movement from Russo until the detective ripped the duct tape off from his mouth.

"Caitlin. Oh God, the pain. I can't even think..." said Russo.

"Don't worry. We'll get you over to a hospital right away," said O'Connell as she reached for the keys hanging on the wall to unlock the handcuffs.

"I'm sorry I came over here," said an apologetic Russo. "I didn't..."

"Tony, be quiet. We'll get you out of here and over to a hospital fast," said O'Connell. She ran back and found her two-way radio on the floor, which had been lost during her gunfight.

"Steve? Steve? Are you there?"

In a matter of seconds, Garden City and NYPD police offic-ers stormed into Weiss' house and down the basement stairs with their guns and rifles drawn. Chief Consoli had apparently radioed ahead to the Garden City police, as dozens of squad cars had already closed off Nassau Boulevard. Two of the officers helped the EMTs carry out Tony Russo into an ambulance. Steve Glover shook his head in disgust after viewing the bodies of both Freddy Weiss and Johnny Merseburg.

"Caitlin, you have some 'spalin to do," said Glover as he attempted a bad imitation of the '50s fictional Cuban TV singer Ricky Ricardo.

"Shut up, Steve," said O'Connell, who was clearly not amused by his lousy impression. "I'm sure I'll get plenty of time with the chief any minute now."

"Well, he's upstairs. But in light of what's happened, maybe he'll cut you a break," said Glover.

"Don't know about that," said O'Connell. "I'm pretty sure that they wanted Weiss alive rather than dead."

"Maybe," said Glover, "although I doubt he was the surren-dering type."

As O'Connell walked towards the stairs leading back up to the main floor, she spotted a crate of unopened records still in their plastic wrapping. They were all the same record: Freddy

Weiss' solo record *Phaedrus*. The basement was officially now a crime scene and nothing was to be touched or removed until further notice. But the detective secretly reached in, taking two copies of Weiss' record and slipping them into a bag Glover was carrying. One was for her and the other for Russo.

Perhaps her rock journalist friend had a better feel for what the late Freddy Weiss was all about but Caitlin O'Connell didn't have a clue. She was too busy hunting down a madman to care about hearing his music. But when the time was right, the exhausted detective would make the time and listen to the music of Freddy Weiss. She wanted to find out for herself if that old quote from Albert Einstein—*the difference between stupidity and genius is that genius has its limits*—was true. The detective was confident, however, that she already knew the answer.

# CHAPTER 30

▼

It was around noon when Detective Caitlin O'Connell walked up the long stairs and into the majestic Metropolitan Museum of Art. The Fifth Avenue museum was a city landmark that she had visited a couple of times in grammar school but it wasn't the sort of place that she gravitated towards later in life. There just weren't a lot of outings that the NYPD made to the local museums.

But O'Connell was going there today not for art but to see her friend, Tony Russo. It had been four months since the Freddy Weiss murder spree had ended. She was aware that Russo was still suffering from a serious inner ear problem aggravated when the "Rock Star Killer" attempted to take the rock critic's life. The email from Russo last week directed her to meet up inside The Met's New American Wing gallery.

The detective followed the museum map and walked to the wing where Russo was waiting. As O'Connell entered the gallery, she could see Russo admiring the American classic painting, "Washington Crossing The Delaware" by himself. The

12-by-21 foot mural by Emanuel Leutze was frighteningly large but every visitor gravitated to the well-known 19<sup>th</sup> century masterpiece.

"Boy, that's some painting. Is there any room in the boat for me, Tony?" said O'Connell as she kissed Russo.

"Yeah, it is," said Russo. "It's probably my favorite in the Met. I'm really not into a lot of that modern stuff."

"I figured that. You're a classic guy. Classic paintings, classic cars, classic rock. But I'm with you on that front as well," said O'Connell. "So why are we meeting here?"

"Well, the art museums are the best places for me right now," said Russo. "The outdoor parks can be a problem with the airplanes flying overhead and construction crews working. And a library, believe it or not, is too quiet and that drives me crazy. So I thought this place made the most sense."

O'Connell sat down on the wooden bench next to Russo. "So it's still there, huh? All the ringing?"

"I still have my tinnitus but it's much better than it was," replied Russo, "and the doctors have been great. But I don't think I'll be going to any more rock shows in the near future. I think it's time I wrote my book—that's a nice quiet activity."

O'Connell smiled. "Quite a run we had for a couple of weeks, huh? I mean for all of that to happen and how we teamed up. In retrospect, Tony, maybe we should have stayed together rather than splitting the work up. You were riding a bit high when you got that info on Freddy Weiss."

Russo nodded his head in agreement. "You know, when my wife Jeanne read about what had happened at the house, that was one thing. But when she went on with me for the first TV interview I did on NBC, she started to break down. I don't think she had any idea of what I was up to while I was working with you. After the interview, man, she got really angry. She said, 'You know you could have left me a widow with kids. Did you ever think of that?' That was hard to respond to. I guess I wasn't thinking straight."

"It happens a lot," said O'Connell, "but I should have known better. I didn't call my chief, I didn't call the local police."

"I know that. But did things calm down a bit with your boss?" asked Russo.

"Yes and no," said O'Connell. "As you know, the media had a field day with how the case was handled, especially having you play detective with me. The chief basically assigned me to some low-level cases but I'm not sure that's for me. I'm a high-energy person and I can't be sitting at some desk checking background stuff all day. I came into work one day and someone had put the Clint Eastwood 'Dirty Harry' DVD collection in my locker. So I think that gives you an indication of what my co-workers are thinking. That I'm a bit of a loose cannon."

"Sorry to hear that," said Russo. "Are you thinking of leaving the force?"

"It's funny you should mention that. I was doing an interview myself for NBC too and the guy doing the interview, who's my age, went to the same high school as me. We got talking for a bit and we ended up going out on a couple of dates and it's working out real well. He's a career guy who never settled down so I think we're getting to that special place."

"Well how about that?" said Russo. "You may be taking the plunge after all."

"At 39, I can still get married and have kids. I know I'm behind in that department but he wants to move quickly as well. I know I don't know him as long as others I've dated but it just seems right. And I'm also thinking of taking up the guitar again."

Russo smiled. "Good for you. So you're off in a new direction. But, man, I had some pretty bad nightmares for a while."

"Yeah," O'Connell replied, "I had some restless nights too. But I'm used to dealing with this crime stuff much more than you are. And what's going on with Tommy Peterson's autobiography?"

"Ha!" said Russo. "I got a couple of calls. One was from Tommy Peterson's mom, one from his ex-wife, another from Bob Wittman from the Winding Roads' management company. They all want all the notes that Tommy gave me but they all want them for different reasons. His mom wants to exclude any reference to the murder, Mary Pat wants to create a hybrid book with her writing about the murder part and Wittman wants to use the notes in a separate book about the band."

"So what did you do?" asked O'Connell.

"I mailed everything I had to Peterson's attorney and told them in a letter I wanted nothing to do with the book. Let them battle it out in court without me," said Russo.

"That was a big move," said O'Connell. "I thought your critic buddy Don Bart told you that it would be a big best-seller if you wrote that book for Tommy."

"Tommy's gone so I really can't ghost write his autobiography. I think I have enough for my own book now anyway," said Russo. "I think Bart was referring more for me to write my own book. I still am doing assignments for Johnny's mag *Rock Forever*, but the new publisher and I don't really see eye to eye. He's more of a sales guy than an editorial guy and his co-owner brother knows less than he does. They're less interested in thought-provoking pieces and more about the tabloid crud. Like the first-hand account I wrote for them about Freddy Weiss? They thought it wasn't scary enough."

"Let's walk around a bit," said O'Connell. "I never come in here." The two former partners continued into the next gallery.

"So I'm getting the feeling that you're not that big a fan of Tommy Peterson anymore?" said O'Connell.

Russo gazed down at his feet as he walked by O'Connell's side. "I know the rock and roll business can be just as cutthroat as, say, Wall Street or pro sports or any level of government. And Freddy liked the high energy jobs. But the thing about guys like Freddy Weiss was that all he thought about was music, night and day. Freddy knew if he made it, he could do this forever. I mean Wall Street's a burnout career, sports you have to have talent and you're done at 40 and in government you're really not making headway until you're past 40. So look at Tommy. I mean he started out when he was in his mid-teens and was coming up on 60 and was still doing what he wanted to do, for the most part, on his terms."

"And Freddy never got that chance," said O'Connell.

"Exactly," said Russo. "Now I'm not saying that the project Freddy was working on back in '69 was going to be better or worse than the other records that all of the other influential artists of his generation. But Peterson squeezed him out because he got a peek at Weiss' demos and decided one less competitor in the marketplace was a good thing. Tommy thought if Weiss and Black Manic Panic were as good as advertised, they would find their own way to make it work without The Winding Roads having to support them."

"Right. But it wasn't up to Peterson to help Weiss' band along anyway, was it?" said O'Connell.

"No, but at the same time I think there was enough room for others to share in the success. Look, all of those great classic rock bands in the Sixties were tough cookies. They supported each other's music publicly while remaining fiercely competitive. To me, it seems that Peterson and Indigo went the extra distance to keep someone out that just wanted a piece of the action."

"I find it interesting hearing you talk like this," said O'Connell. "Especially knowing how long you and Tommy were friends."

"I think that's the hardest part, Caitlin," said Russo. "I knew him for three decades. I wasn't a relative of his, a big record label guy or a fellow rocker. But I thought Tommy was comfortable enough to share everything with me when he was putting his book together. To me, that was a big story he could have gotten off his chest. But maybe he didn't care about it anymore, which was his right. But after what happened, I don't think I'm the right person for his book."

"I understand," said O'Connell. "And what about Freddy's recordings and those reels he kept. Did they get tossed away?"

"I know you're going to think I'm crazy," said Russo, "but I had a talk with one of Weiss' relatives. They sent all the stolen *Timelessness* demo reels back to the record label along with his solo reels. I spoke recently with one of the surviving members of Black Manic Panic and they are inviting me down to a remixing session with a top record producer from New York. With all the buzz about Freddy Weiss, BMP is apparently getting back together. I'm going to create some liner notes for their 'never released' record. They think they can make a fortune after what happened. Bad press is good press, right?"

"Boy, that's a bit creepy," said O'Connell. "I mean the guy almost kills you and you're going to write liner notes for his posthumous CD? That's not freaking you out?"

"You would think but it doesn't," said Russo. "Hopefully the other three BMP members will go through the reels, re-record some tracks and make this into something memorable. It's good therapy for me anyway to tackle Freddy Weiss head on rather than run away from him. And since we're doing the mixing in New York City, I want you to come down to the sessions. The band said it was fine if you did."

"Really?" said O'Connell. "I will take you up on that offer, Tony. You know, I only got to meet Freddy Weiss for a few minutes and under terrible circumstances. I'm curious to know what was on those demo tapes that made him so crazy."

"Be careful how you phrase that, Caitlin," said Russo.

"How so?" said O'Connell.

"It wasn't the recording of the music that made him nuts. It was the business of music that got to him. Freddy had exactly what Tommy had at the same time, but Tommy didn't share his toys well with others when all Freddy needed was a little help. Once Tommy took Freddy's toys away, that's what happened, according to Freddy."

O'Connell put her arm around Russo as they towards the museum's restaurant. "You're an interesting man, Tony Russo."

"Well, my dear, over lunch I will explain the meaning of life," said Russo. "If you have time."

Caitlin O'Connell put her arm around Russo's waist. She had heard the meaning of life explained by her father, her priest in grammar school, her college bandmate, and her boss over at the police station. It was interesting how it was only the men in her life who claimed to have all the answers to life's mysteries. But the detective knew that one more explanation wasn't going to hurt her, especially if it was coming from her new buddy Tony Russo.

# T.P. Autobio
## summary notes excerpts (late '60s section)

It didn't exactly happen overnight but soon after the reviews came in for <u>Everything Is Nothing</u>, the radio stations jumped all over it and spun it to death. As that happened, we went from being a well-known band to a household name mega band. And none of us were ready for it.

I did think we deserved it, though. We had busted our ass all through the Sixties, playing the high schools and colleges, small pubs, radio rooftop shows, even a birthday party or two. We gained momentum after an early slot at Monterey in '67 and hung in there in '68, which was a total disaster after Kenney lost his voice for three months and I broke my left hand playing basketball after we recorded <u>Blank Slate</u>. Our management, who worked us to death in '69, more or less 'bribed' the Woodstock promoters to get us onto the bill at the very last minute. The gigantic crowd loved our set and motivated us when we headed back to The Hit Factory in New York City with the new material.

The songs on <u>Everything Is Nothing</u> flowed out of us so easily that the band was again convinced this record was going to be the BIG ONE. As always, I was cautiously optimistic. The last two albums I had written I thought were killer records from where I was sitting. They did well but they barely went gold. But when <u>Everything Is Nothing</u> was released in the fall of '69, the theme, songs, timing, whatever spoke to everyone. And it was like we became a completely new band overnight. We were now up there with The Doors, The Beach Boys, The Who, The Rolling Stones, and the rest. Not The Beatles, of course. Nobody was in their class.

But with that record came the problems that continued to follow us. Everyone wanted to get into our camp and join the party. The shady drug dealers, the willing groupies, the nasty critics, the crooked cops. Even a couple of religious folks who had invented their own religion that made it fit into their hedonistic needs. Personally, as long as those sycophants didn't interfere with my money or interrupt my creative time, I didn't care. John, Steve, Andy and Mike all had their personal demons to battle and they each dealt with their own issues by themselves.

I wouldn't say it was the beginning of the end but we couldn't go back to the way things were. Unfortunately we did steamroll past some friends of ours along the way; even family had to take a backseat for a bit 'cause we were coping with our newfound fame. Another downside was that we were now individuals living apart and playing in a band rather than a five-in-one band traveling in a van. John was now landing bit roles in movies, Steve was in the *gossip pages every other week for causing some ruckus, Mike was using the new money to open a restaurant and Andy became a part-owner in a professional hockey team. Maybe it was a bit of paranoia but I was the only one focused on the music.*

*Looking back, I don't think I would have gotten through that record or anything else if I hadn't met Indigo then. The second she came into my life, she put a smile back on my face after it disappeared for a couple of years. Aside from battling with the band, I was fighting constantly with my ex Mary Pat about the kids and money with no end in sight. When that record took off, suddenly I was the richest guy in the world to Mary Pat and she let the press know that I was 'forcing' her and the kids into poverty. Why nobody realized that most families in poverty don't attend private schools and live in seven-bedroom mansions was beyond me.*

*But Indigo became my protector and savior and helped me negotiate everything. She took care of the personal business things that I wanted to avoid, as I'm not a good paper person. She developed new relationships with the press and the record label so that they became more like associates rather than adversaries. That's why Indigo has always been by my side—the studio, the walks, the tours, the meetings, everything. I know that there have been plenty of people that believe Indigo has been a bad influence on me or that she took away some of my independence.*

*If anything, Indigo encouraged me to think on my own. In the past, if John wanted to do something that I disagreed with, after a certain period of time I would just give in because I couldn't take it. Once Indigo came into the picture, however, I refused to back down. Sometimes the fights in the band got ugly and I was ready to walk out the door. Indigo would then calm me down and explain to me the art of compromising. My mother hated Indigo because my mom was used to me coming to her when things got bad.*

*But Indigo always has known what was best for me—past, present and future. She is me and I am her.*

# (ROCK FOREVER—Issue #11)
# This Road Is Closed—Tommy Peterson
# (1949–2004)

### By Tony Russo

When I broke into this God-forsaken music industry as a teenage rock journalist roughly three decades ago, there was no MTV, no Internet, and no hip-hop music dominating the radio. The teenagers' choice of music back then was rock, and there was only one musician that personified everything I loved about rock music: Tommy Peterson, the inimitable guitarist and songwriter for The Winding Roads. Explosive, insightful, mysterious and witty were just a few of the many descriptions attributed to the talented New Yorker who was tragically murdered last month at age 58 in the place he often called 'home'— his recording studio in Manhattan. I was fortunate enough to call him a friend and his death leaves a hole in my life as well as the rock music community.

Born and raised on Long Island, Peterson's musical talent told him early on in high school that he was not destined to be an accountant or a firefighter. His classmates, keyboardist Mike Going and drummer Andy Garger, met up in 1963 and started jamming to Buddy Holly songs in Going's garage. A few months later, singer John Kenney and bassist Steve Mars met the other three at a party they were playing at and The Winding Roads were formed. With controversial rockers of the Fifties such as Chuck Berry and Jerry Lee Lewis influencing Peterson and his band mates, The Winding Roads became as creative and fearless in both the studio and live as England rockers The Kinks and The Who.

Technically speaking, Peterson wasn't the smoothest or fastest guitar player but he made up for that by utilizing complex jazz chords in a rock song format. Peterson's songwriting also became more expansive and dynamic as the band continued to develop their individual styles throughout the Sixties. Their relentless touring during that tumultuous decade, which included appearances in all three major rock concert events (Monterey, Woodstock and Altamont), paid off with the release of their stellar concept record, 1969's *Everything Is Nothing*. The two-record effort that chronicled a couple's journey around the globe for the meaning of life hit home with fans that were looking for answers of their own. On the same scale as other influential records of its time such as The Beatles' *Sgt. Pepper's* and The Who's *Tommy*, the record lifted the band out of insolvency and into classic rock megastars throughout the Seventies.

Married early in his career to photographer Mary Pat O'Callaghan, he had two children with her. But Peterson's rock and roll lifestyle soon led to divorce. Shortly after their split, he finally met his longtime girlfriend/artist Indigo, who exposed the songwriter to many things beyond the rock and roll world. Although the dynamic pair was not as outspoken as John Lennon and Yoko Ono, both Peterson and Indigo were active on many environmental causes and often seen at many New York City protest rallies.

Peterson did not escape controversy. His recent murder (and Indigo's murder a few days later [see cover story]) by obscure Sixties songwriter Freddy Weiss was apparently an act of revenge fueled by a decades-long accusation that Peterson sabotaged Weiss' career in 1969, which culminated in Weiss' death by police during a shootout a few days after Indigo's murder. And in 1974, when Winding Roads bassist Steve Mars succumbed to alcohol and hypothermia a short time after being "asked" to leave the band, several people accused Peterson as the "cause" behind his long-time friend's death. Other news items, such as an ugly paternity suit in Europe and a run-in with a New England mob family, also kept the rocker in the headlines.

The long time New Yorker began to reevaluate his life and career after The Winding Roads slowed down and began working more on his solo career, releasing the very successful *Table For One* in 1978. Peterson finally freed himself from the giant behemoth that The Winding Roads had become, finalizing matters with the band's last studio effort, 1989's *Goodnight.*

During the last decade of his life, Peterson stretched himself artistically beyond the confines of the music industry by writing a couple of fictional books, composing an Off-Broadway play and displaying his photographic skills at small art shows in lower Manhattan. Peterson once said in an interview that, "I think more of us need to explore different avenues in our life. We have opportunities in front of us but I'm always running into people that do one thing their whole life and that's it. To me, that's not much of a life at all."

As a friend who was assisting him on compiling his thousands of notes for his unfinished autobiography, I believe Tommy Peterson did everything he set out to accomplish during his exciting yet abbreviated life in the fast-paced world of rock and roll.

Rock on, Tommy. Wherever you are.

# THE WINDING ROADS DISCOGRAPHY

*Welcome To The Winding Roads (1964); Talking Pictures (1965); Letters From Mary (1967); Blank Slate (1968); Everything Is Nothing (1969); Black Wine and Red Nights (1971); Live At Pier 42 (1973); My Country (1975); Golden Days (1979); Moonshine (1981); Greatest Hits (1984); More Live Than Dead (1988); Goodnight (1989); Alternate Detours: The Complete Winding Roads (1995)*

# TOMMY PETERSON DISCOGRAPHY

*Breaking Out (1975); Table For One (1978); Open Window (1982); Tommy Peterson Live in NYC (1985); Whistle (1987); Extras and Samples (1990); Cover Me (1993); The Almost Best of Tommy Peterson (1995); The Fire Within (1997); Untitled (work in progress; TBA);*

# Rock & Roll Reference List

Here's a list of people, places and things mentioned in the book affiliated with rock music. Albums are in *italics*, songs are in 'quotes' and music folks are in **bold**. The easy thing would be to describe each item but research them yourself. How else will you learn?

Advent, **Aerosmith,** Altamont, **The Animals,** Apple Power Mac G5, **The Beatles, Chuck Berry,** Billboard Magazine, *Black and Blue,* **Black Sabbath,** *Bleach,* **Blondie, Marc Bolan, John Bonham, Bono, David Bowie, The Backstreet Boys, Jackson Browne, Eric Burdon, Ricky Byrd, The Byrds, David Byrne, The Carpenters, Mark David Chapman, Eric Clapton, The Clash, Kurt Cobain, Joe Cocker, Cream, Mötley Crüe, Puff Daddy, Roger Daltrey, Ray Davies, Clive Davis, Deep Purple, The Doors, Bob Dylan, The Eagles, Ahmet Ertegun, Mark Farner,** Fender, **Foo Fighters, Pink Floyd, Ben Folds Five, Alan Freed, Liam & Noel Gallagher, Genesis,** Gibson, **The Grateful Dead,** Gretsch, The Hard Rock Café, **Debbie Harry, Heart, Don Henley,** The Hit Factory, **Buddy Holly,** iPod, 'I Will Follow', **Mick Jagger, The Jam, The Jimi Hendrix Experience, Billy Joel, David Johansen,** 'Johnny B Goode', **Brian Jones, Janis Joplin, The Kinks, KISS, Phil Lesh, Jerry Lee Lewis, John Lennon, Led Zeppelin,** Madison Square Garden, **Madonna,**

978-0-595-81271-4
0-595-81271-6

Printed in the United States
34883LVS00003B/4-15

9 780595 812714